BILLIONAIRE ROMANTIC

JULIE CAPULET

Noah Maddox is a hot as hell billionaire who, as it turns out, is impossible to resist. He's also an absolute beast in bed...

Details I didn't know, of course, when my best friend sets me up on a blind date with Noah "Steel". It's obviously a fake last name. But then again, so is mine.

From the moment we meet, we're like magnets who can't resist each other's pull. The blind date lasts all night. Then the entire weekend. The best of my life, if I'm being honest.

But when Monday morning comes too soon and we both have to go back to work, I'm shocked to find out that my sexy blind date is actually Noah Maddox, the evil CFO of the company that's planning to take over my late father's struggling investment business. The takeover will cost me my job, every cent I have and, worst of all, my beloved apartment.

If only I hadn't spent the weekend in bed with the devil, cashing in my V-card and throwing all caution to the wind…because how does a girl say no to all those mind-blowing orgasms?

I thought he was perfect. Until I find out he's not the

sweet-and-dirty-talking dream man I fell for at all, but a shark who's about to take everything I have.

It's entirely Noah Maddox's fault that my life is now in shambles. I don't care how drop-dead gorgeous he is, the man is obviously a nightmare.

So why is he obsessively trying to prove to me that he's the most devoted, head over heels billionaire in New York?

And how am I supposed to resist the hot romantic who has already stolen my heart?

Billionaire Romantic is a steamy billionaire romance starring a hopelessly romantic CFO and the sassy blind date he'll do absolutely anything to keep. Each book in the New York Billionaires series is a complete standalone with a sexy fairy tale HEA.

New York Billionaires

Julie Capulet LLC

BILLIONAIRE ROMANTIC
New York Billionaires
Copyright © 2025 by Julie Capulet

BILLIONAIRE ROMANTIC

1

NOAH

As I weave my Ducati through the usual madness of New York City traffic on a Wednesday morning, I make a decision.

It's safe to say I'm different to my brothers in many ways. My brothers always describe me as the "nice" one out of the four of us. The "romantic" one. The one who's most likely to believe that something like true love actually exists, despite the train wreck of our parents' legacy. I'm the one who supposedly still has faith that good things can happen. According to my brothers, they're the cynics and I'm the optimist.

But the universe has a twisted sense of humor. Because over the past few months, all three of my cynical-to-their-bones brothers have fallen head over heels in love.

I'm happy for them. I'm over the moon that fate has somehow proved them wrong. That each one of them is capable of falling so hard and so fast that all three of them had rings on the poor girls' fingers before they even knew what hit them—and, in at least one case, or possibly more, they've already knocked up their wives-to-be because they're incapable of thinking about anything except getting that particular job done.

And I, the only one of us who isn't—at least wasn't—allergic to the words "relationship" and "commitment," am still thoroughly unattached, disillusioned as fuck and pissed off that my "optimism" has obviously jinxed me.

Here I was, thinking it was worth waiting for The One. I'm the only brother who hasn't relentlessly slept my way around the island of Manhattan because I idiotically convinced myself that I'd prefer to actually *feel* something for the person I'm having sex with.

No longer. That game plan has done nothing except provide me with endless disappointment.

The decision locks into place, right here on the corner of Fifth Avenue and East 34th Street.

I'm no longer going to wait for that one elusive, perfect woman who never shows up for me. My brothers can drool all over their one-and-onlies, freeing up the New York dating pool for yours truly.

Fuck it.

I'm going to go out and find myself some unsuspecting girl with fake tits and dollar signs in her eyes, like they all seem to do. I'm going to stop pretending that the woman of my dreams exists.

And I'm going to get fucking laid.

It's been way too long.

It's not that I *can't* get women to fall in love with me. I can, very easily. The only problem is, most of them are after me for my looks or, obviously, my money. My brothers and I happen to be some of the wealthiest and most successful investors and businessmen in New York City. So was our father and so was our grandfather. It's well known that a shitload of zeroes are attached to my many bank accounts, which of course is a super-powered magnet for every woman with a heartbeat.

Being the fool that I am, I've mostly avoided meaningless sex because I was hoping I would find…well, *meaning.* Love. *True* love, even. The kind of love you'd kill or die for. The kind that completely blinds you to everyone and everything except the one true love of your life.

The kind of love that staunchly, relentlessly eludes me.

Unfortunately, my brothers know me too well. I *am* a fucking romantic. I *crave* it. I want to fall in love so badly I feel like I can't breathe some days. Like there's a huge hole in my heart and my life that only she—a phantom lover who probably doesn't even exist—can fill.

It's depressing. And infuriating.

Where the fuck is she?

I've clearly got it all wrong. The only people around here who are falling in love are the die-hard skeptics who don't even believe in it.

I pull my Ducati into my parking space in the private

parking garage under our building so abruptly I can smell burnt rubber.

It's another point of difference between me and my brothers. All three of them prefer to be chauffeured around in their limos. I like the chaos of the traffic. The soundtrack of the city reminds me that there's a world outside our glass box that doesn't give a damn about our investment portfolios or our share values.

Not being a slave to city traffic also means that on mornings like today when I'm earlier than usual, I can stop in to get coffee at the coffee shop around the corner from our office that has proven to be by far the longest relationship of my life.

It's the first place I became a regular when I started working in the city, long before Cash poached me to be CFO of his company.

Our family company, Maddox Equities, which owns its own city block including the skyscraper that houses the company's headquarters, is directly across the street. I started working at Maddox Equities the day after I graduated from Harvard, as we all did. As we were all expected to do, whether we chose it or not.

Alexander, the oldest of the four of us, still runs the family business. It was always his destiny to be CEO.

Cash and our father butted horns too often to work together easily and Cash wanted out. Since there were more crazy family dynamics than even *I* knew what to do with, especially before our father died—and I'm considered the "diplomat" and the steadying force in our family —Colton and I jumped ship as soon as Cash offered it.

The skyscraper across the street from the main hub of my family's empire happened to be for sale. So we bought it and began building Invested Enterprises from the ground up. It's been incredibly hard work. We've worked our guts out and weathered more than a few storms, but it's all been worth it. Business is most definitely booming.

So the Daily Grind and I go way back.

I pull off my helmet and secure it to the bike, glancing at the watch Alexander insisted on gifting me last Christmas. A Rolex. It's not usually my style to wear half a million dollars on my wrist but even I have to admit it's a nice watch.

It's almost nine.

As I make my way out onto the street and around the corner, I vaguely notice as traffic stops and the rush of the crowd hurries across the crosswalk. But something's holding them up. A frail-looking elderly woman wearing a bright yellow headscarf is being very nearly trampled by corporate assholes. She's hunched over a cane, barely a third of the way across. The light's about to change.

Despite my mood, I can't help myself. I walk over to her. "Excuse me, do you need some help?"

Her eyes narrow as she stares up at me. "If you're thinking of mugging me, Buster, I don't carry cash and my diamonds are locked up in my son's safe in Hoboken."

I like her feistiness. "I promise I'm not going to mug you. I'm Noah. Let me help you across the street."

"Enid," she replies, sizing me up and apparently finding me trustworthy enough. When I offer her my arm, she takes it.

We start our slow, slow journey across the street. The traffic light turns green before we're even halfway and horns blare. Enid grips my arm tighter, using my support and her cane to take another step. "If I wasn't holding onto you, dear, I'd be giving those morons the finger."

This makes me smile. "Maybe let's not give any pre-caffeinated New Yorkers the finger until we get you safely across." A driver revs the engine angrily and screeches past us.

"Assholes. Everyone is always in such a rush these days," Enid sighs, continuing at her snail's pace.

"Big plans today, Enid?" I ask, in an attempt to distract her from the cab driver who's wound his window down specifically to yell obscenities at us.

"Oh, you know, the usual. Judge Judy and Jeopardy with my sister Mabel, then maybe I'll go shoplift some Tums later. Just kidding, they're locked up like Class A drugs these days. Mabel is ninety, a spinster and ornery as hell, but she insists I visit her every morning. And I have to be nice to her in case she dies first. She keeps threatening to leave her fortune to her hairless cat Nigel."

I didn't think I was capable of laughing this morning

but Enid has proven me wrong. "Quite the agenda you've got there, Enid."

We finally reach the other side.

"Are you going to be okay getting to your sister's, Enid?"

"Oh yes, I'll be fine from here. I've walked to Mabel's every day for fifty-seven years. I could do it blindfolded." Enid steadies herself. "I'm sure you have places you need to be, looking like you do."

"I'm happy to help if you need it."

She squints up at me. "Whoever gets to keep *you* is one lucky lady. If only I'd met you when I was a looker in my twenties."

"You're still a looker, Enid."

She cackles nostalgically. "And you're a good liar. And very charming. Not to mention tall, handsome and well-dressed. And *built*, good Lord. Tell your lucky lady she better appreciate the catch of New York City." She pats my arm and begins shuffling away. "Have a good day, Noah. And thank you."

"My pleasure." I watch for a moment as she makes her way down the street, concerned she's going to be knocked over by a guy who's reading on his phone and not looking where he's going. But Enid's ready for him. Before he can barge into her, she gives his leg a well-aimed thwack with her cane. He jumps back, letting out a little howl. Limping and glaring, he gives her a wide berth as he hurries away.

Enid's going to be just fine.

I make my way back across the street and hear someone yelling my name. Colton steps out of his limo. "Tell me you did *not* just help an old lady cross the street."

I don't bother confirming or denying.

"Dude, you're a walking cliché," Colton laughs.

"And you're an ego-inflated asshat, but we love you anyway." We make our way inside the Daily Grind.

"Hi, Noah." It's one of the baristas who knows me by name. Because I have to give a name for my order. I make a point of asking theirs because I come here a lot and it seems like the right thing to do. I happen to know her name is Elli with an i, because it's how she introduced herself. She blinks blue-tinted eyelashes at me.

"Hey, Elli with an i."

Her smile is doe-eyed. Colton elbows me but this girl is so not my type. She has piercings all over her face and a goth look that's never really floated my boat. "Can I get you your usual, Noah?"

"Make it three, please."

They always get my order first, no matter how long the line is.

Elli hands me my coffee, making a point of placing it in the cardboard three-cup-holder so I can see she's written her number on the side. "Thanks, Elli."

She bites her lip, blinking at me again. "Bye, Noah. See you again soon, hopefully."

We get out to the street and Colton is still laughing.

"Jesus, she might as well have had 'Fuck me' tattooed across her forehead. You should call her. Getting up close and personal with a chick with *that* many piercings could be interesting."

"Give it a rest, Colton."

"Just go with it, bro." Colton keys us into our private elevator. "You're too wholesome for your own good." Not entirely true. There's a side to me my brothers definitely know nothing about. "Unless the rumors are true," he smirks.

I don't bother taking his bait. "You're in a good mood," I observe.

"It's called getting laid, Noah. You should try it sometime." Ever since he met Lila, Colton has been insufferably *happy*. Cole was always the fun-loving Casanova of the pack of us, but now there's a new, fervent light in his eyes which, considering both his past and his usual devil-may-care attitude, is probably the best advertisement for true love I've ever seen.

"I'm not taking your place as the family fuck-boy, so you can drop it," I tell him. Then again, that's exactly what I just made a decision to start doing.

The elevator dings and the doors slide open. Directly opposite the doors is one of our main boardrooms, which Cash happens to be walking into. "Better than the Maddox Monk," Colton replies.

Which of course is all the invitation Cash needs to join the conversation. "How's the vow of celibacy going?"

"Fuck off," I tell him, handing him his coffee as I walk past him into the boardroom.

"Good morning to you too." Cash smiles at how easy it is to rile his usually Zen brother. He sets his coffee and some folders at the head of the table, pulling out a chair. "The mood hasn't improved, I see."

"My mood is none of your—or his—business. Let's just get on with the meeting you insisted we come to."

More grinning, but Cash tunes in to the fact that I'm really *not* in the mood for their rainbows and unicorns happiness right now—because they happen to be right. My epic dry spell is getting *way* out of hand.

2

NOAH

Cash slides a folder toward me, then to Colton, getting straight to the point. "All the info I've got so far on Ashton Holdings."

Colton starts leafing through the paperwork. "Who are they?"

"They're a smaller investment firm that had a reputation for hitting a series of lucky scores around fifteen or twenty years ago. The founder, Henry Ashton, had an almost prophetic knack for good timing. But he refused to modernize with the times and their profits have suffered for it."

"Then why do we want to go anywhere near them?" I glance at the file on the table but leave it closed. I want to hear what Cash has to say before I look at the numbers and dismiss it immediately.

"Because they're undervalued. The founder died around six months ago of a sudden heart attack."

Colton looks up from the file he's leafing through. Fathers dying of sudden heart attacks is something we can relate to. "Who's running the company now?"

"Ashton's kid. Who's completely inexperienced. It isn't going well for them. Their shares have plummeted."

I recline back in my chair a little, taking a sip of my coffee. I'm trying to remember if I've heard of Ashton Holdings but I'm coming up blank. "Sounds like a disaster."

"At the moment, it is. But *we* know what we're doing and with a small amount of effort we could turn it around. It's a special little company with huge potential."

It's a weird thing for Cash to fixate on, considering everything we've got on our plates with our own company. "Why are you so interested in it?"

"We could most likely get a good deal. We should act quickly though. A few other companies are starting to smell the blood in the water. Abundance Investments is one of them."

"Ah." That explains it. A few months ago when we were investigated for an insider trading incident—which never happened and eventually blew over—the CEO of Abundance, Chad Bentley, poached a few of our clients, convincing them we were untrustworthy. So there's a reason Cash wants to one-up Abundance. "There has to be more to this than just revenge."

"There is. There's a shitload of money to be made here, Noah. *If* we act fast." Cash's competitive streak is fired up. "And it would be satisfying to piss off Chad, admit it."

"Has Chad made an offer?" Colton continues to leaf through the paperwork.

"Not yet." When Cash is in one of these moods, he won't accept anything other than getting the deal done. "I say we go in with a strong offer," he says. "One they can't refuse."

"If they're in that much of a bind, we should start low," Colton suggests. "They might take any reasonable offer that comes along."

"I don't want to be outbid," Cash insists.

I'm aware of their ongoing conversation, but for a few minutes, I say nothing. I'm distracted by the decision I made this morning, which feels like a black cloud casting its dark shadow over my future. It's kind of heavy to basically have given up on true love. I always thought it would just...*find* me. In a lightning-strike, out-of-the-blue kind of way that felt like it was meant to be.

No such luck.

And my current dry spell is making me feel like I might throttle someone and/or spontaneously fucking combust.

I take a deep breath, exhaling slowly. And non-obviously.

It's good. Everything's fine. I'm resolved now. I'm doing it.

I'm going to…do something. Hunt down the most desirable option, then I'm going to get down and fucking dirty until I can find some sense of relief—with no strings attached. No feelings. No commitments. Nothing. Just pure, hot, take-no-prisoners sex. With…someone.

Who, I have no idea.

I try to look on the bright side: I'm young, hot, rich as fuck and have women calling me up every day of the week begging me for a date.

Most of them are people I've already let down gently, women I dated once or twice but felt nothing for. Surely *someone* out there has to have enough appeal to make me forget I'm not in love with them for one goddamn night.

I'll figure it out.

But even though I'm determined now, part of me feels…*sad.* Losing your faith in something as important as finding the love of your life is sort of depressing.

"Yo, Noah, are you in the room?" Colton waves his hand in front of my face.

"What?"

Cash leans back and folds his arms, staring at me like he's mildly concerned. "What's going on with you? Are things really that bad?"

"I don't know what you're talking about," I bluff. Like the question bores me.

But my brothers are nothing if not relentless. "Dude,"

Colton says, "call the number on your coffee cup. Let off some steam with Emo Girl."

I sigh. "Fuck no."

"Okay, then one of the other six girls who were swooning over you in the coffee shop. Even *I've* heard through the grapevine that you're some kind of beast in the sack, bro. You hardly fly under the radar in this neighborhood."

At least Colton knows how to almost make me laugh. "Jesus, Colton."

"What can I say, the women in this town talk. And, trust me, it's horrendous to listen to. Either way, I'm sure you have no shortage of offers."

I glance down at my phone. Which is, in fact, lighting up and full of text messages and ignored phone calls. The few women I do date tend to stalk me for a long time afterward. I don't ghost women or treat them badly and apparently that's a novelty. They beg me for months—sometimes years—to give them another chance.

My brothers don't get this. Sure, they're in love now, but all three of them have pasts that are strewn with broken hearts. None of them ever had a problem being an asshole.

Me, on the other hand, I just can't bring myself to do it. The tears. The begging and the pleading. It's downright torturous. I just can't…*hurt* them.

"This is worse than I thought," Colton says, making a

call before I can stop him. "Sloane, could you come in here, please?"

"For fuck's sake," I mutter.

The last thing I need is Colton's extremely gossip-fueled assistant to be in any way consulted on my dismal love life. But in Sloane waltzes, willowy and sassy as fuck, leaving the door wide open. "Good morning, everyone." To Colton, "What can I help you with, boss?"

"What was the name of that dating app you were talking about yesterday?" Colton asks her.

"You've got to be kidding me." I stand up to leave.

I almost get the idea this whole thing was planned though, because Sloane is standing in the doorway, like she's intentionally blocking me. She launches straight into her pitch. "It was written up in the New York Times as being *the* new big thing. The success rate for the matches is unprecedented. *Everyone's* joining it. It's called Lucky In Love."

"Not interested, Sloane," I growl, hoping she'll take the hint and let me out the door before I have to somehow physically move her myself.

"It's supposed to have these really intelligent biomet-rics that get amazing matches," Sloane insists. "It doesn't go on things like, oh they both like dogs, let's match them up. It's way more nuanced than that. The algorithms are incredibly sophisticated. They deep-dive into your internet footprint. The app has a success rate of eighty-seven percent. Which is amazing. You should try it, Noah."

I glare at her. "Maybe *you* should try it, Sloane."

"I would but I'm seeing someone at the moment." She blinks up at me, her excitement at the prospect of match-making for me glinting in her brown eyes as she firmly stands her ground. My glare slides to Colton. Then Cash.

Of all of them, I thought Cash might be my ally, but he says, "You should give it a shot, Noah."

I'm being ambushed.

"*Totally* worth a shot," seconds Sloane.

Colton picks up his phone and starts tapping away.

"Don't you fucking dare—" I grab for his phone but he's already out of his seat, dodging me as he types. I outweigh him and he knows from experience—from the few times he's pushed me too far, like he's doing right now—that I can kick his ass. But I'm hardly going to chase him around the goddamn table.

"What harm can it do?" Cash asks me.

"This is *Colton* setting up a dating profile for me. Are you hearing yourself?"

Colton gives me a smug grin. "There. You're signed up. They'll come back to us for more info over the next few hours. Then we can sit back and watch the matches roll in. And don't worry, I gave you a fictional last name."

"I'm going to annihilate you for this."

"You won't want to." Colton gives me an earnest look.

"You'll be too busy getting laid and falling in love. I'm only doing this because it *works*, Noah." But I can tell he's ready to run if I lunge for him. "We want you to be happy."

Happy.

Colton's phone is already pinging with incoming messages. He's set the whole thing up so fast I'm wondering again if this was pre-meditated. "They're going to email me the follow up questions shortly. If there's anything I don't know, I'll ask Cleo."

"Here to help!" my obviously-already-in-the-know assistant chirps from her desk.

Wonderful. So the entire office is in on it.

Cleo rushes in, high on her enthusiasm for their shared new quest. She grins at me. "Morning, boss."

She never calls me "boss." "Cleo."

Cleo, Sloane and Colton start poring over the app like it's Christmas morning. "Oh my god, Colton, this profile is too good. Noah *Steel?*" Sloane and Cleo erupt into laughter.

Just when I thought this day couldn't get any worse.

Cash gives me a guilty, sympathetic smile but does nothing to stop their chatter. "Who knows, you might find the girl you've been searching for."

"I think we both know that's about as likely as Ashton Holdings being the investment of our dreams." I take my opportunity while they're distracted and walk out.

3

Lucky

As I WALK into the lobby of my apartment building at exactly 6:02 pm, I notice my surroundings in weirdly acute detail.

It might be because of the adrenaline overload still coursing through my veins after a series of insanely intense meetings. Those stern lawyers, fuddy-duddy financial advisors and pissed-off shareholders really are a buzzkill, holy hell. Talk about doom and gloom. They had nothing to offer me except dire predictions about our company's plummeting share values and were basically manifesting its imminent demise. My cortisol levels feel like they're spiking through the roof right now.

I'm also taking in every detail because I know I might not be seeing the familiar lobby of my beloved building for very much longer. Which makes the luxuriousness of it all really pop.

As the day's meetings pointed out with devastating clarity, it might only be a matter of weeks before I lose everything I have.

Where the hell am I going to go?

I notice with fresh eyes how impressive the white marble walls are, with the ever-trickling waterfall gleaming in the early evening sun. The giant bouquet of fresh-cut flowers that always sits on the front desk is especially decadent today, like something straight out of a hedonistic scene from a Caravaggio painting. All we need is a few bowls of decaying fruit and a couple of hot Italian, tousle-haired toy-boys. The concierge on duty waves to me as I walk to the row of elevators.

I've always appreciated the luxury, of course. Maybe there have been times when I've taken it for granted, only because it's all I've ever known. But not often.

And if I don't somehow figure out how to turn my father's business around—a Herculean task—my livelihood, my home and any safety net I might have is all going to slip through my fingers like sand.

I've lived in this building since I was four years old. I remember the day we moved in, clear as a bell. My mother was wearing her new pink Chanel suit and as soon as she saw the Juliet balcony, she burst into tears. She was *so* happy—as any New Yorker would be, no matter how new they are to it, when they land an apartment as cool as ours.

My parents met when my father hired my mother as

one of his assistants. She was twenty and had just arrived from Ireland to interview for her dream job. He was thirty-four and fell in love with her on the spot, hired her, fired her (he made up for it) so he could marry her. The two of them took their vows less than three months later. I arrived seven months after that.

My father wanted to name me Emerson, a family name, but he begrudgingly had to settle on using it for my middle name. My mother insisted on naming me Lucky. It's on my birth certificate and everything. Lucky Emerson O'Callahan Ashton. On all the paperwork related to my father's business though, I'm named as L. Emerson Ashton. Which I didn't realize until after he died, and it almost made me laugh.

He never got his way when she was alive—he loved her too much to argue with her.

My mother was wild and whimsical, with bright blue eyes and strawberry-blond curls that always looked a little windblown, like she'd just stepped out of the neon-green farm-scape of County Cork. Which she had.

I don't know how they managed to fall in love with each other, the two of them were such different people.

My father was raised in New York, the youngest son of an old-money (depleting at an alarming rate) family.

Chester Emerson Ashton, my great grandfather, was originally from Pennsylvania and made his money in steel. A *lot* of money.

Which my grandfather, Chester Emerson Ashton II,

managed to burn his way through impressively quickly. He lived the high life and had a fantastic time spending all of Daddy's money while making very little of his own. He bought a sprawling three-story penthouse apartment on the Upper West Side and a vacation home in Southampton. But his business ventures tended to be less than spectacular. Several of them failed.

First the Hamptons home had to be sold. Soon after, the penthouse.

By then his two sons had attended all the best schools, enjoyed a privileged upbringing and were starting businesses of their own. Chester III, my uncle, took after Chester II and was too used to easy wealth to be hungry enough to keep it and grow it. He divorced twice (two more big blows to the family fortune) and eventually became a dissatisfied mid-level banker who drank and medicated himself into an early grave.

Chester II's younger son, my father, was more focused. He'd always been a quiet, introverted and slightly eccentric child who clearly saw the writing on the wall.

I don't know if my father might have, these days, been considered "on the spectrum" or not, but he was one of those people who lives and breathes numbers. Like you see in the movies where numbers are scrolling in front of the vision of the mad professor or the unhinged savant and they can't help but be obsessed with them. I'm sure he was a genius, if anyone had bothered to test him for it.

Realizing early on that his family's money was all but

gone, my father set out to make his own. He taught himself how to invest from a young age and had an uncanny knack for finding undervalued needles in spreadsheet haystacks. He started his fund when he was eighteen and worked on it obsessively. By the time he was in his late twenties, his fund was a force to be reckoned with, had landed squarely on the Wall Street map and every greed-monger in a suit wanted a piece of it.

But my father had two weaknesses. One, he insisted on doing things his own way. Which was staunchly old school. He refused to follow new trends or even update his technology, preferring to use the same techniques he'd used when he was poring over the financial pages in his adolescent attic bedroom instead of hitting the yacht club with Chester III.

His other weakness was my mother. When she wanted a red sports car, even though she'd only ever driven on the Irish side of the road and never once in New York, he bought her one. When she wanted to spend the summer in the Hamptons, he rented her dream house, right on the water (buying it was too much of a liability; he'd seen what a money pit it had been for his father). When she insisted she was fine to drive us out there and he would meet us on the weekend, he allowed her to follow her whims.

And when the car rolled three times off the side of the Long Island Expressway, killing her instantly, while I, a sheltered four-year-old who *adored* my mother and had never spent so much as a moment apart from her, walked away without a scratch, everyone said "Lucky" was the right choice.

After my mother died, my father became even more of a reclusive number-crunching workaholic.

I was of course lost without my mother.

But with my brigade of new Irish nannies (I remember begging my father with devastated tears: *please* can they be Irish), a personal chef and a driver who took me to and from my trendy, progressive private all-girls school (my mother's choice, which he honored all the way through), I slowly adapted to life without her. My Irish nannies read bedtime stories to me while my father worked. I made friends and lived, for the most part, aside from the gaping hole in my life without her (and mostly him), a happy life.

My father did not. Without my mother, he lost his purpose, his whimsical, strawberry-blond sunshine and the center of his universe. In the end, I think even the numbers slowly crushed him. He had no interest in pivoting or making the most of new opportunities. It was like he was frozen in time.

I tried to comfort him as best I could. But I think I reminded him too much of her. I look almost eerily like her, except that my hair is blond instead of strawberry. If I'm being honest, I think it broke his heart a little more every time he looked at me. I know he loved me, but his grief overpowered it. He spent more and more time working and slowly going down with his own ship.

Now, I wish I'd asked him more questions about his business, of course I do. Especially since I was always going to inherit it, even if I never expected it to be so soon. I can see more clearly now that he could have used my help. He *should* have used my help.

Like him, I have a head for numbers—although I was never even close to his league—while also having my mother's ability to think creatively and her insistence on looking for the bright side.

Then again, I doubt my father would have taken any advice I might have been able to give. He was too entrenched in his own grief and his own deep, labyrinthine mind.

I sigh as I unlock my door. Anyway. Shoulda woulda coulda.

I set my keys in their little silver bowl on the front table, drop my bag and slip off my shoes.

"Hey, Luck!" my roommate Grace calls from her room.

"Hey, Gracie."

I can't help but notice—as always, but especially tonight—that the light in my apartment really is to die for. It's something New Yorkers *always* appreciate.

I'm *really* going to miss it.

4

———

Lucky

GOING over to the window seat, I sit against the soft, plush cushions, taking it all in. It's been a day.

The quaint view of my private little outdoor balcony garden that looks out to the night-lit skyscrapers is such a rarity in New York City. I love the old-style water tower that sits on top of the building next door, like it belongs in a chic European movie. A small slice of Parisian charm right here in the middle of the Manhattan skyline. I know exactly how lucky I am to have it.

And how devastated I'm going to be to lose it.

When the clouds are moody and the sun is low, there's nowhere more beautiful. Golden rays flood my living room, catching the darkly colorful hues of the Persian rug and casting a soft glow onto my carefully curated bookshelves. Even my indoor plants—stubborn survivors of my recent neglect, because I've been so busy

—look like they belong in an upscale home decorating magazine.

In fact, my apartment has been featured in a few home decorating magazines. I'm into decorating. It's the thing I do to de-stress, when I can manage to take a break from working or studying. My own little form of escapism. Honestly, few things bring me as much joy as scouting through antique stores and cute homeware boutiques and finding some little gem. My father couldn't have cared less so I took it upon myself to create the magic. And it *is* magical.

This apartment is my own personal slice of heaven. I can't imagine living anywhere else.

It's where she was happiest.

It's where I'm happiest.

Unfortunately, I *have* to imagine it. Because if today was any indication of what the future holds, I'll be packing my bags by the end of the month.

My roommate bounces into the room. Grace and I met the first day of grad school at NYU. We were both just starting our MBAs. We sat next to each other at one of the orientation lectures and started talking. We've been practically inseparable ever since. She moved in with me the day after my father died, just over six months ago.

"Long day?" Grace sits at the other end of the window seat.

"Yes." I could reply, *awful, terrible, scary, horrible doomsday.* But I'm trying to find some silver lining in all this. Speaking the words only makes them more likely to come true. "But it's better now."

"I'm very happy to announce that I've got the solution to all your problems—okay, maybe not all, but definitely a few—right here in my hot little hands."

Grace is holding her phone, grinning like she just… wait a minute. "Why are you *glowing*?" I demand. "And why are you dressed like that?"

I'd just finished the first semester of my MBA when my father dropped dead. I had to put my studies on hold to work full-time as the newly-appointed CEO of my father's company—much to the shock and horror of the grouchy Board, but there was nothing they could do about it. There was nothing *I* could do about it either, even though I was far from ready. It was all very black and white in the will.

Grace is still studying and spends most of her time in sweats with her messy bun pinned into haphazard place with a pen. But not today. She's dressed in skinny jeans and a tight-fitting pink sweater. Her cheeks match her sweater and her dark hair is very…*clean*, hanging over her shoulders in glossy but slightly chaotic waves.

She's still grinning at me. In fact I'm not sure I've ever seen Grace look so *elated*. But she also looks…like she just spent the afternoon rolling around in bed and then quickly smoothed her hair not-quite into place. "Grace? What's going on?"

She laughs, and there it is again. A kind of pure,

uncut happiness I'm not sure I've ever seen concentrated in this way in my best friend before. "I just got laid, that's what's going on."

I blink at her. "*What?*"

"You heard me."

"When? How? With *who*?"

She sighs deeply, closing her eyes and leaning her head back against the carved wooden frame of the window seat. "By the dreamiest dream man in the entire freaking world, that's who."

"Seriously? *Grace.* Who is he? How did you meet? Why don't I know about any of this?"

She opens her eyes, those flags of pink on her cheeks getting even pinker. "Luck, it was a-*may*-zing."

"It was? But who is he?"

Grace and I have bonded over many things. One of those things being that we're both twenty-three and we both are—or *were*—virgins. We're picky. We've discussed this. We're waiting for not just any old fling, but something special. "Luck, it was better than anything I could have imagined."

"Holy shit, Grace," I laugh.

"I *know*," she gushes.

"But...how? When did you meet this guy? I didn't even know you were dating anyone." It's true I've been insanely snowed under with my new job lately and she's been studying non-stop, but we still take the time to talk at least a few times a week.

"I met him today."

"You met him *today*? Where?"

"At Bryant Park. We'd arranged to meet there."

"Arranged? How?"

"*God,* Luck. You *have* to try it. I met him through this new dating app everyone's been talking about. Remember that girl in our Organizational Behavior class named Hattie? She told me about it. This app has, like, gone viral because the algorithms are so accurate. They somehow make really good matches."

"You met him on a *dating* app?" *And you jumped straight into bed with him?*

"He's also getting his MBA. At Columbia. He's in his final semester. We'd agreed to meet for lunch. Luck, he's so freaking *hot*. I was like, are you *kidding me*? *This* is my blind date? And then after we had lunch and a drink—two, actually—he invited me to check out the apartment he just moved into. It's insane. He was offered a job even though he hasn't graduated yet and there was a signing bonus that was so big he bought himself an apartment. He closed on it just last week. The only piece of furniture he's bought so far is a futon. It's a one-bedroom in Hudson Yards. Can you *believe* that?"

"No."

"It's freaking *true*."

"Hot, loaded *and* employed? He sounds like a fictional character."

"He *looks* like one!" Grace exclaims. "He's handsome

but he's also nice. He was in a long-term relationship and they just broke up, like, two months ago. He broke up with her. He said they had different ideas about the kind of future they wanted. She moved back to Kansas or somewhere, because she hates the city. He wants to live in New York. It's always been his dream and he's worked really hard to get here. He's sort of serious and academic and he wears these nerdy little glasses that look so cute on him. He has a close-knit family upstate and he played hockey at Cornell. So he's, like…I don't know how to explain it, Luck. He's *perfect*."

"Wow. A hot hockey-player finance nerd. He *sounds* perfect."

"I think he might be. And then he kissed me and one thing led to another. I knew we were taking things at warp speed but I figured why not? I might never get another opportunity like this again. So I went with it."

"Holy shit, Grace. And it was…okay for you?"

"It was more than okay." Grace leans her head back and closes her eyes again. But then she opens them and they're wide with emotion. "I had the first three man-induced orgasms of my life and they were *spectacular*."

"*Three?*" This makes me laugh a little, and that's something, considering the day I've had. "Yay, Gracie. I'm so happy for you."

"Thank you, Luck."

"Are you going to see him again?"

"Yes. Tomorrow. He had to go to a company dinner

tonight but we're going to meet up again tomorrow night."

"Wow," I say again.

"So no matter how shitty your day or week or month has been, I have the solution."

I laugh again. "A dating app? That would definitely *not* solve my problems. I'm thrilled for you, sweetie, but the last thing I need right now is a relationship. *Or* a fuck buddy."

"Don't knock it 'til you try it, girlfriend. Trust me, it lives up to the hype and then some."

My stomach growls and I remember I haven't eaten since breakfast. "Have you eaten? Let's order in."

"Nice try, L. Emerson." I told Grace about my dad's official title for me and she found it hilarious. She picks up her phone. "I'm making you a profile."

5

———

Lucky

"Don't you dare." I get up and wander into the kitchen. "I'm getting a glass of wine. Do you want one?"

"Of course I want one. I got laid today!"

Smiling at her excitement, I pour two glasses of ice-cold Pinot Grigio. Carrying them back to the window seat, I set them both on the raised marble-topped table my mother bought at an antique store in the Village, just a week or so before she died. Every single thing in this apartment has a story, but this piece of furniture is one of my favorites. "I didn't even ask you what Mr. O's name was."

"Ethan. Ethan Patrick Malone."

"Ethan Patrick Malone. He definitely has Irish in him. Which makes him a good catch. And he even told you his middle name, which is a good sign. It means he's honest."

"If you say so." She's typing on her phone.

"By the way, it's a good thing Ethan Patrick Malone has an apartment. Because there's a very real possibility we're both going to be homeless soon."

This gets her attention. She stops typing and looks up at me. "It can't be that bad, Luck."

"Gracie," I tell her honestly. "It is."

"But you're Lucky Emerson O'Callahan Ashton. Luck follows you wherever you go. It can't happen. Something will work out. It has to."

I sigh heavily. "The truth is, the company was in a lot more debt than I knew. Storms have been brewing for a while now. My father never told me how bad things had gotten."

Grace takes a contemplative sip of her wine. "I know I'm only an aspiring CFO at this stage, but is there anything I can help you with?"

"I wish there was. "

"You're smart, resourceful, and stubborn AF. You'll figure it out, Luck."

"I honestly don't know what to do. No matter how hard we try to crunch the numbers into something that works, they refuse to cooperate. Even when we sell—*if* we sell—I'll personally still be in the red by, oh, almost exactly as much as this apartment is worth."

"He didn't put the apartment in a trust?" She seems shocked, just like I was. Of all the things to overlook.

I shake my head a little, trying hard not to burst into

tears. "Must have slipped his mind. It was in his name, and now it's in my name."

There's a stubbornness I know and love behind her empathy. "Well, if anyone can figure this out, it's you."

I'm usually a die-hard optimist, but today my look-on-the-bright-side-no-matter-what attitude has taken a hit.

Grace clinks her glass against mine. "Hey. Come on. This is just the universe testing our resilience. If we have faith that things are going to work out better than we ever could have imagined, then they will. Girl, if we can't Excel our way to billionaire status, we'll just have to manifest our way to it."

Grace is big on manifesting. I'd accuse her of being woo-woo about it, but she actually *has* achieved amazing things and if that's how she wants to pitch it to herself, then why not.

"I'm living proof that it works," she insists. "If I hadn't manifested my way into your swanky apartment, right now I'd be living in a chicken coop somewhere near Bangor."

"I think that had a lot more to do with a shitload of hard work than mere manifestation." I shrug. "But I'll drink to it anyway."

She smiles and there's a sadness there as she tries to make light of our situation. "I'm a champagne-taste-on-a-lemonade-budget kind of girl and it would be morally reprehensible of you to pull me out of my squalor only to throw me back into it again. I won't let you."

Grace is originally from a small town in rural Maine. Her parents went through a bitter divorce when she was ten and she was passed back and forth between her parents'—as she calls them— "shacks." Neither of Grace's parents had any money. They both were deeply mired in poverty. According to Grace, this was because they had a poverty-focused mindset. They didn't *believe* there was any other destiny for themselves except to be poor. They lived off food stamps until Grace was old enough to get an after-school job at the library, where she read every book she could get her hands on about how to get rich.

Grace was determined not to follow in her parents' footsteps. She decided a long time ago that she didn't want the life they had. So she set her sights on making as much money as possible by focusing obsessively on studying finance. She managed to get a full ride in scholarships to NYU for her undergrad and is now halfway through her MBA (with substantial student loans). Despite the scholarships, she still has a lot of debt, is usually cash-strapped and is often barely getting by. But the fact that she's here at all is a testament to her amazing work ethic, her belief in herself and her grit.

"I just don't see how I can fix this," I admit.

"Okay. Take a breath." Grace sets her almost-empty glass back on the table. "I have a plan. We're going to *will* this to work out."

"We are?"

"Yes. We're going to order some food, drink more wine and we're going to focus all our energy on pretending your apartment is fully paid off and your business has had a sudden turnaround. Meanwhile, we're going to distract you from worrying about all of it by setting you up with the perfect match."

"I can get on board with the first half of your proposal, but I am not in the right frame of mind right now to deal with some disastrous blind date."

But Grace won't be swayed. "Honey, that's exactly the kind of negative mindset I was wallowing in. For *years*. Then I cowgirled up, uploaded my profile and look at me now! Still riding my endorphin rush from three back-to-back *orgasms*, thank you very much. Don't be such a stick in the mud, Lucky. *Let* yourself be positive. That's when good things start to happen. You *need* a date. It's perfect timing."

One thing about Grace is that, once she makes up her mind about something, it's impossible to talk her out of it. But I'm still not convinced.

"Listen to this." She starts reading to me. "'New Yorkers are heading in unprecedented droves to the latest matchmaking app, which is redefining digital romance. Lucky in Love combines algorithmically-sophisticated compatibility metrics with a healthy dose of serendipity. Think of it as a virtual Cupid, but unlike its competitors, one that doesn't throw darts in the dark. New Yorkers of all ages are finding what some are calling their uncannily perfect match—so many, in fact, that wedding planners have never been in higher demand.'" Grace tips back the rest of her wine. "See? We're doing it. We're creating a profile for you."

"Wedding planners? Don't you think you might be rushing things?"

She ignores me, typing fast.

"Grace, I don't have *time*—"

"I'm not listening to your excuses. Because they're the exact same ones that held me back. And once I finally let go of them, I met the cute-hot hockey nerd who I literally can't believe is real."

"And I'm happy for you. But sex isn't going to solve my problems."

"Maybe it is! It would at least take your mind off all your woes. The universe *responds* to shit like that, Lucky. If you're focused on how good you feel, the universe will pour more of that feeling into your life. It's just the way things work."

I roll my eyes.

"Surrender to the process. What better distraction is there in the world than a super-hot man to wine and dine you and take you to bed? Trust me, it's exactly what you need." More typing. "You're a Pisces, right?"

"*Grace.*"

"Are you open to dating outside of your astrological compatibility?"

"*Grace!*"

"What? Just humor me. If it doesn't come up with a match, you can go back to your no-sex drudgery and nothing will have changed. Either way, it'll at least take your mind off the looming apocalypse for a hot minute."

I try again. "It's not good timing."

"Too late." Grace grins and holds her phone up, showing the screen that says *profile uploaded* in cheerful all-caps.

"I can't believe you."

"I named you Lucky Irish." The grin gets even wider.

A weary laugh escapes. "Lucky *Irish*? I sound like a leprechaun."

"I know you use the word in most of your passwords. So it therefore has meaning to you. It's surrounded by good juju. Can I use this photo?" She holds up a photo of me she took a few weeks ago when we had a picnic in Central Park one Sunday afternoon. One of those New York days that was too beautiful to stay inside. In the photo, the sun catches the different colors of gold and platinum in my hair and I look…happy. An emotion I haven't been up close and personal with all that much lately. "I love this photo of you. You look hot. And dreamy."

"Grace," I groan, but there's a laugh brewing in my chest because this whole thing is ridiculous. "I don't want to go on a blind date right now."

"Babe, it's not like things can get much worse. The only thing you have to lose is your virginity."

That corny line does it. Our emotions are running high and we both burst into hysterical laughter.

I know all too well that things can *always* get worse. But hey, if Grace's new glow is anything to go by, maybe there's something to her theory after all.

"More wine," she splutters between breaths. "We're going to need more wine."

6

NOAH

The spreadsheet on my screen is a sea of red, like a digital battlefield where all the numbers have been slain. I blink and rub my eyes, half-hoping that a second look will magically resurrect those digits into black. But nothing happens.

If it were up to me, the idea would have been scrapped days ago. Cash, however, has a strange fascination with this sinking ship, which is the only reason why I'm contemplating throwing them a life jacket. Because if I don't rein him in, he'll do it anyway, and we'll end up paying way too much.

I call his number.

He picks up on the first ring. "Hey. What's the verdict?"

"The verdict is no." Even as I'm saying it, I know he

won't listen to my voice of reason. "My advice would be to leave it and move on."

He's quiet for a second. From the hum and occasional honk in the background I can tell he's in the back of his limo, on his way to his next meeting. "We're good at fixing things, Noah. We don't run from challenges."

"I agree. We can navigate anything that's thrown at us." I think about the insider trading fiasco and how we managed to get through it without much help from our CEO. It was at a time when Cash was so distracted by a random woman he'd met in Hawaii but couldn't find, I thought the entire company might tank while he searched for her. Then she showed up out of the blue—we'd hired her without realizing who she was—and Dusty turned out to be the love of his life. So we forgave him, of course. But I know as we're talking that we're both well aware that it was Colton and me who managed to pull I.E. back from the brink. It's one of many reasons I know he'll listen to me. "Ashton Holdings is an unnecessary risk. It's one we don't need."

"Our line of business is all about risk, brother. It's literally how we make money."

"I'm aware of that, Cash." I rub my hand across my jaw. "But my job is to analyze whether the risk comes with a big enough reward. And this one isn't guaranteeing that."

"Only because it's been mismanaged for a long time. Surely you can see the potential here, Noah."

"Yes. I can. But it's not worth the asking price you've given me. Cut that number in half and then maybe we can do something with it. We need to go in lower."

Cash pauses but finally relents. "Okay. Let's offer fifteen million then."

I'm glad he's finally seeing some sense. "For the record, I still think it's a bad idea. But you're right, there's potential here. And we can work with fifteen."

"You know, I'm surprised," Cash drawls. "I thought you'd jump at the opportunity to help a poor little undervalued company with huge potential and a tragic backstory. You know that kid is having a bad month." The kid who inherited the company and is now acting CEO is listed as L. Emerson. "We're about to make his day."

"Either that or ruin it."

"I respect your opinion on this, Noah, you know I do. I want you to be happy with the numbers."

"Happy is overstating it. But for that price, we can make it work."

"Okay. Good. Thank you, Noah. I'll give this L. Emerson a call tomorrow morning then."

"Keep me posted."

We end the call and I lean back in my chair, rubbing my eyes. Fuck, why does it feel like it's the longest day ever?

Usually I love my job.

I thrive on it.

But the decision I made this morning is coloring everything.

I've given up.

No, I've decided to be realistic. There's a difference.

Is there?

The door of my office opens, and Colton walks in with his phone held out, like it contains something rare and breakable. "We have a match, ladies and gentlemen!"

I narrow my eyes at him. "What?"

"Feast your eyes upon your perfect woman. Ninety-eight point two percent compatibility. You should probably just skip dinner and get hitched already." Cole grins, holding his phone out to me.

I read the name in the middle of the screen. "Lucky Irish? You've got to be kidding me. What is she, a leprechaun?"

"Either that or your pot of gold."

"Jesus, Colton. This has to be a fake."

Cole laughs. "Your name is fake too, Mr. Steel."

"I can't believe you named me that," I grumble.

"Sloane and Cleo wanted to go with Noah Grey, given your reputation, but I reined them in."

"What reputation?"

"Apparently one of the girls knows someone you went out with."

"So?"

"They call you 'the beast'." Colton's grinning from ear to ear.

I ignore him as best I can. "Anyway, I'm not dating Lucky Charm."

"Lucky Irish. Before you refuse, at least look at her photo."

"Colton, would you drop it already?" This is starting to piss me off.

"Dude, I'm trying to *help* you. We need to do something to improve your atrocious mood. The app has suggested the two of you meet at a bar called Hopeless Romantic tomorrow night. It's new. It's only three blocks from here and has so far received only five star reviews. One tap and you're booked for tomorrow—*if* she taps too, which I'm betting she will."

I stack and file the paperwork I've been staring at all afternoon. "The app tells you where to meet?" I guess that's mildly interesting.

"The algorithms figure out the place where you're most likely to feel comfortable based on your profiles."

"You're wasting both our time." I sigh, feeling surly. "She probably wouldn't even show up."

Colton smirks. "Oh, she'll show."

"How do you know? Are you pretending you're me and chatting her up or something?"

More laughter. "I would never do that." He's enjoying my misery immensely. "Besides, the app doesn't have a chat function. It's designed to get people to meet in real life. No texting until after you've met."

"I'm not doing it, so you and Cleo and Sloane can stop meddling in my love life and work on your own."

"My love life is already perfect, thanks for asking. Yours, however, has room for improvement." Colton sets his phone down, sliding it across the desk. "At least look at her before you refuse."

Grumpily, I pick up his phone, glancing at the picture. Zooming in a little.

Holy hell.

She's smiling. Her hair is white-blond and wavy, hanging almost to her bare, warm-looking shoulders. She has olive skin and eyes that are a bright, off-neon shade of blue. Her teeth are white and neat-looking and her lips are full and pink. She's very…*colorful.* There's something wholesome about her, but with an edge. You get the feeling she's got a wild side. She looks, in a word, *luscious.* Against my will—and at the worst possible time imaginable—my mouth waters and my cock thickens. *Fuck.* Behind her, the trees and faraway buildings are framed against a blue sky. She's in Central Park, on one of those perfect New York days. "This has to be fake. Nobody looks like this."

"Photos are scanned to see if they're AI-enhanced. This one isn't."

"It tells you that?"

"Yep."

"This is real?"

"Completely real."

I zoom in a little further. *She's fucking gorgeous.* You can tell she's both sweet and sassy just by looking at her. She's curvy and has a quirky style, reminding me of one of those fifties pin-up girls with a modern twist.

She's absolutely flawless, is what she is.

Colton is highly amused by the way I'm staring. "All you have to do is click confirm. Then if she also clicks, it's a date."

"She hasn't confirmed yet?"

"Not yet. But the algorithm only made the match around ten minutes ago. Give her time. Cleo and Sloane chose the photo and they both said you look hot."

"Which photo?" I ask, hating myself for suddenly caring about my profile on this ridiculous app.

"That one of you on your deck at the Hamptons house. Cleo and Sloane said you look normal and approachable."

"Approachable?" I cringe, still staring at Lucky Irish's picture.

"Yes. You don't look like a lunatic, in other words."

"Oh." I'm too distracted by the photo to reply further.

"At this stage, both of you have only given non-identifying information. But we do know she's lived in New York her whole life and she works doing something in finance."

"She doesn't look old enough to be in finance."

"She's probably having the same doubts you're

having, Noah. She'll be just as surprised as you that she's found someone who's compatible with her. So, what do you say?" His eyes lock onto mine, the humor fading into something that could almost pass for concern.

I hesitate, flicking my gaze from Cole back to Lucky Irish.

"You might as well meet her," he says. "*Look* at her. She's fucking gorgeous."

I frown and I can't name the emotion that's suddenly coursing through my veins. *He can see that too?* Of course he can. Is this suddenly feverish pull…*jealousy?*

"Can I have my phone back now?" he grins.

"No." I'm not done staring at her.

"So," Colton says, almost gently. "You like what you see. All you have to do is click to confirm and you can meet her tomorrow night. You've got nothing to lose, bro. Just *do* it."

Unfortunately, he's right. I *don't* have anything to lose. Tumbleweeds are currently rolling through the deserted wasteland of my romantic life. I also, I remind myself, this very morning, made the decision to give up on finding love and work instead on getting fucking laid.

This girl who's smiling beatifically at me in all her sun-lit glory could in fact be the answer to all my disillusioned prayers. The fact that I'm practically hard from one glance at a total stranger in a slightly out-of-focus photo on a tiny screen confirms that my dry spell has sent me spiraling into the outer orbits of severe sexual frustration. Something needs to be done about it.

"Live a little," comes my brother's relentless encouragement. Which at this point I might even be grateful for. He brought me Lucky Irish. "We all know you're the steady one. The reliable one. The one who keeps everyone grounded and always has our backs. Well, this time I've got your back. The app is legit, the girl is real and you've got no plans tomorrow night. Cleo already checked your calendar. I've got a good feeling about this one, man. I want you to find what I have."

I look up at him, a little shocked by the genuine emotion coming from my playboy-turned-smitten brother. "Wow, Cole. That was—"

"Deep?" he interrupts, the smile returning to his face. "Yeah, Lila says I have layers. Like a sexy onion. So, are we booking this date or what?"

I glance back at Lucky's profile and then back at Cole. His eyes are still filled with that new light—love—that has changed him for the better. The kind of love I've never experienced. It's the kind of glow *I* want to feel. Just once.

"All right," I say, punching the confirm button. "Let's see if Noah Steel has better luck than Noah Maddox."

7

Lucky

I wake up feeling groggy after a fitful sleep. Checking my phone, it's 7:02 a.m.

My dreams were awful. Spreadsheets bleeding real blood. Me, a lost little orphan like something out of a Dickens novel, begging on the streets and peering into derelict buildings to find shelter from the rain.

I get up and make myself a cup of coffee, willing the nightmares to fade out, which they mercifully start to do. I take the coffee out to my balcony. Grace is still asleep.

Sitting on the cushioned couch that gets the early morning beam of sun, I start to feel a little better. My climbing plants frame the view, giving the space a romantic charm. A breeze stirs my little herb garden and I can smell the thyme.

I always feel closest to my mother when I'm out here. Even though I can hear the honking traffic and the sounds of New York City waking up below me, this space always feels so peaceful. Up here, nothing can touch me. I can almost imagine that the world *isn't* crumbling into a pile of rubble all around me.

I come out here when I need to feel her presence. To think about what my life might have looked like if she was still in it. And to remember how it used to feel when she was infusing everything with the unfiltered love she always surrounded me with.

Mama, if you can hear me, please help me. Help me figure out what to do. Help me make the right decision.

Looking out over the city skyline, to the European-looking water tower on the roof of the building next door, I take in the familiarity and comfort of the view. And I contemplate my options.

One, I can try to bring in one or more shareholders who will help me service the debt for a share of the company.

The problem with that option is that the company has a *lot* of debt. *Eighteen million dollars* of it. A number I prefer not to think about too closely. Once upon a time it was worth seventy million. But times have changed.

I'd have to offer the *majority* of the company's shares to make it an attractive enough proposition. Which means I'd lose control. Which means I'd be at the mercy of the new shareholders. They might sell the company, possibly for an unreasonably low price.

Two, I can sell the company myself and try to get as

much as I can for it. But even if I sell at market value, I'll be left with so much debt I'll have to sell my apartment.

Best case scenario: I sell the company for way above market value for it and get to keep my apartment. This, however, is about as likely as me getting a new pet Pegasus to fly around on at sunset every evening.

Three, I can wait until we go bankrupt and lose everything.

And my fourth and final option: I can hope that by some miracle our share prices suddenly skyrocket.

But let's face it, in today's economy, I might as well wish for Ireland to drift across the Atlantic and park up next to the Statue of Liberty, for leprechauns to hand me their pot of gold as they build a quaint but sturdy bridge that connects my balcony to the green fields so I can visit my mother's grave whenever I feel like it. And my father's too, once I get over being mad at him for not putting the apartment in a trust, like any normal person would have. (My mother told my father to not even consider burying her ashes anywhere but in the County Cork dirt or she'd haunt him for the rest of time. In the end, I decided to bury my father's ashes right next to hers because he loved her more than anything and by then there was no one left in his family to complain about it.)

So, no matter what I decide to do, all four options add up the same.

I'm going to lose everything.

I honestly don't even *care* about the company. I'd gladly *give* it away if it meant I could keep my apartment.

My apartment is my life, my world and it contains every memory I've ever had. I had hoped it would also contain my future. *And my own little girl, with strawberry-blond curls and eyes the color of a County Cork summer day.*

But that's not going to happen. Keeping my home, no matter how many times I crunch the numbers, is not on the list of my options.

The thought makes me once again want to pound my fists on the ground and burst into tears.

But I don't. I can't. I haven't cried since before my mother died. Not even as a grief-stricken four-year-old. Not a single tear.

Instead, I *use* my sorrow. I channel it into figuring out what I'm going to do.

Everything *in* my apartment will have to be sold too, of course.

All my mother's beautiful pieces and all of mine. Each one has all the milestones of my life etched into the marble and the wood. Soon to be sold to the highest bidder.

I'm trying to find a bright side in all this because it's what I do. But none are coming to mind at this exact moment.

Maybe it'll be *good* to start completely over. Yes. A refresh. Selling the place that contains all my tragic memories will give me a new, fresh beginning, free from pain. Wide open.

Except that it also contains the beautiful memories. The happy ones. The ones full of love.

Anyway.

Reality bites, as they say.

It'll be *fun*, I try to convince myself. I'll find a swanky new place to live. Somewhere cool and funky. Modern and artsy instead of old and history-seeped.

I won't be able to afford to continue with my MBA for a while until I figure out how I'm going to survive at the most basic levels, but who cares? Maybe the MBA was never meant to be.

Maybe, instead, I'll become an…interior designer. *Don't you need money to do that?*

Or…a writer, of articles about home decorating. *As if. You've never written anything besides spreadsheets and financial analyses.*

Or…an entry-level clerk at a bank. *That's more like it. I mean, who would even hire you? You inherited a company you're about to lose. Hardly impressive.*

Damn it.

I sigh, get up, take a shower, get dressed and pour myself another coffee. I'm about to start drying my hair when my phone rings.

I check the screen. Unknown caller.

"Hello?"

There's a pause. Then the deep, strong voice of a

man. One brief question tells me he's extremely self-assured and also pushy. "Is this L. Emerson Ashton?"

"Yes, it is."

He sounds almost flustered. "You're not quite what I was expecting."

"You thought L. Emerson was a man? Yeah, I get that sometimes."

"Right. Forgive me. Ms. Ashton, my name is Cash Maddox. I'm the founder and CEO of Invested Enterprises." Cash's voice is smooth, oozing a smug charm that immediately puts me on edge.

I recognize the name, of course. Invested Enterprises is well-known as being at the top of the New York heap. They get written up all the time in the financial papers. It's run by three extremely successful brothers—who have been called some of "New York's most eligible bachelors." They used to work for their family business, Maddox Equities, one of the most profitable investment companies of all time, before going out on their own. Cash Maddox must be one of those brothers. It's a little intimidating. "What can I do for you, Mr. Maddox?"

"I was very sorry to hear about your father's passing. My father also passed away suddenly so I can relate to how difficult that must be."

"Oh. I..." I wasn't expecting him to say that. It catches me off guard and, after the nightmares and the harsh early morning realizations, it hits me hard. But I hold my voice steady. "I appreciate that."

"I'll get straight to the point, Ms. Ashton. We're interested in buying Ashton Holdings. We're prepared to make a cash offer. We've drafted the offer and a contract, which I'd like to present to you and discuss in person. Are you able to meet with us on Monday morning?"

Holy shit. Could this be it? The answer to all my prayers?

These guys are big players with a lot of money to spend. "What's the offer?"

"As I said—"

"Mr. Maddox, if you could let me know what you're offering, I can then confirm whether or not it's worth meeting." I'm used to dealing with overconfident men. And I need to know.

"Fifteen million."

I swallow. *Fifteen million.*

Ashton Holdings owes eighteen million. My apartment is worth three million—or, on a good day maybe 3.2 minus broker fees, which are insane. The lawyers will also have to be paid. That means that I would just about— maybe—break even. Or possibly be several hundred thousand in the red with no income and no place to live.

Six months ago I'd never even *thought* about the kinds of numbers I'm casually discussing right now. With a billionaire, no less. But circumstance forced me to get up close and personal very quickly with the fact that I was personally staring down the barrel of a shitload of debt with an unnerving amount of zeroes at the end of it.

I'm about to lose my *home.* Is it too much to ask to at

least have a tiny bit left over so I can at least *try* to start again?

To do that, I'm going to need to play hardball with one of the biggest sharks in Manhattan. I know I won't get the number I'm about to ask for but fuck it. "I'm sorry, Mr. Maddox, the lowest I could possibly go would be twenty million." I'm thinking about taxes, maintenance, insurance. And no income.

"Ms. Ashton, Ashton Holdings currently owes 18.3 million dollars and it hasn't made a profit in almost two years."

"I'm aware of that, Mr. Maddox." *18.3?* Where'd that extra three hundred thousand come from? And why am I inclined to believe Cash Maddox's estimates are more correct than my own accountants'? "At its highest value it was worth over seventy million and we're confident we can restore much of that value with new management."

"New management? You're referring to yourself?" Like it's a joke.

Prick. I feel my Irish temper flare and it's just what I need. "As a matter of fact, yes. My father was not forthcoming with all the numbers before he passed and I can admit there has been an adjustment period. But the company has huge potential and I'm determined to realize it."

"It's a sinking ship. I'm offering you a lifeline."

Actually, that's not a lifeline at all. It's a one-way ticket to rock bottom. And I'm not prepared to give in that easily. "You must see some of Ashton Holdings' potential too, Mr. Maddox, if you're prepared to purchase it, holes and all."

There's a pause, and when he continues I get the feeling he admires my fighting spirit. He may not realize I'm fighting because I'm about to be destitute. Or maybe he does. "I'll have to talk to my CFO. He's been very firm about the fifteen million dollar offer. But he may be—if we're lucky—negotiable. How about you come in on Monday morning and we can discuss it."

Just the thought makes my heart feel like it's about to pump its way out of my chest. Two or possibly all three pit bulls versus little old me. But surely they expected a little bit of back and forth. They've come in with a low offer and no doubt they're expecting me to counter it. It's not like they can't *afford* to put a measly five million more into the pot. The Maddox brothers are famously worth multiple billions each. "That would be fine," I say stiffly. "But please be aware that yours isn't the only offer on the table."

"Ah, so Abundance already offered."

He knows about that? "Yes." I can only hope he doesn't know they only offered ten million. An offer I wouldn't even consider.

"I'm afraid I'm tied up all day today or I'd move the meeting forward. Ms. Ashton, are you able to confirm that you'll hold off on accepting Abundance's offer until after you've met with myself and my CFO on Monday?"

Is this a trick? If I say yes, will I be admitting Abundance made a much lower offer? Anyway, the damage might already be done but I have no choice but to forge ahead. "Yes, I can do that. I'm still in discussions with Abundance's CEO," I bluff.

I can't tell if I can hear amusement in his voice or if I'm imagining it. "Great. I'm confident we can come up with a number you're happy with, Ms. Ashton. *If* we can talk my CFO into it, that is. I was prepared to offer more, but he won't budge. He's stubborn as all hell. You and I have our work cut out for us." Is this some kind of scare tactic? At this point I'm dreading meeting with his evil CFO. "How's ten o'clock on Monday?"

"That's fine."

"Do you need the address?"

"No. I know where you are." Everyone knows where they are. They're the most sought-after company to work for in New York City and are written up at least once a week with glowing testimonials about how great it is to be a part of their young, hip, talented team.

"Perfect. See you then, Ms. Ashton. Enjoy your weekend."

The line goes dead before I can even say, "You too." *Jerk.*

8

After another grueling day at work, by the time I get home it's after six.

I open the door of my apartment and find a bottle of champagne on ice sitting on the kitchen island. As soon as Grace hears the door slam closed, she bounds out of her room. She's wearing a pink dress that hugs every curve, light make-up and her hair hangs long and wavy over her shoulders.

"Wow," I say. "You scrub up really well, roomie. You look gorgeous."

"Getting ready for my hot date. Ethan's taking me out to dinner at Via Carota."

"Oh, I've heard such good things about that place."

"Me too."

"What's the champagne for?" I shrug off my coat.

"Are we celebrating that you're about to get wined, dined and laid again?"

"Yes. But we're also celebrating because so are you." She pops the champagne and pours two glasses, handing me one.

I take a sip. "Are you going to tell me what you're talking about or do I have to guess?"

She brings up something on her phone and hands it to me. "A ninety-eight point two percent match, girl-friend. I've never heard of one being that high before."

"Match?" It's starting to dawn on me.

"Feast your eyes on Noah Steel."

"Noah *Steel?*" I laugh. "You're joking."

"It's probably not his real name, just like Lucky Irish isn't your real name. But who cares? *Look* at him."

Still laughing, I glance at the photo on the screen.

I stop laughing and zoom in a little.

Wow.

"Right?" Grace is watching my reaction with glee. "He's freaking *hot.* And he's already accepted the date."

"He has?"

"The app set you up at a new place called Hopeless Romantic. It's a boutique hotel but it's got this trendy little bar and bistro downstairs. He's agreed to meet you there tomorrow night. Seven o'clock sharp."

"That's so soon." But I can't tear my eyes away.

He *is* hot. It's a stop-traffic kind of hotness. His hair is a rich chestnut brown. He's very handsome, but what holds my attention most of all is his eyes. They're a striking shade of blue. With light crinkles around them as he smiles. He looks *nice*, is my first impression. Like he'd hold a door open for you. But he's also got this darkly sexy, manly thing going on. You get the feeling he wouldn't be *too* nice. There are layers there.

He's outside on what looks like a deck with the wide open blue sky that matches the color of his eyes and wispy clouds behind him. He might be at a beach somewhere. The photo looks natural, not like it's been staged for social media. It looks real and unposed.

"See?" Grace is grinning at me. "All you have to do is click 'accept.'"

"But I know nothing about him," I protest, despite the fact that my eyes are still glued to his photo.

"And he knows nothing about you, except the info that was required, which the app keeps confidential."

"It does?"

"Yes. You have to meet him to find out more about him. That's the idea."

"What if he's weird? What if he's a psycho killer or something?" I can admit he doesn't look like a psycho killer. He looks like a normal, well-adjusted, successful person. The shirt he's wearing is a nice one. It's open at his throat, revealing his tanned, corded neck and a hint of chest hair.

Help.

"If he is, then you politely take your leave and you

never have to see him again. He doesn't know your real name or anything about you." Grace squeezes my shoulder. "Take a breath, Luck. It's one date. You don't have to do anything other than show up, have a drink with him, then decide if you like him or not. No drama. No stress."

"But…what will we talk about?"

Grace laughs. "God, has it been so long since you've been on a date that you even have to ask that? Don't answer, because I already know the answer."

"Yeah, I haven't been on a date in…a while."

"I know. I've known you for a year and a half and I don't think you've gone on a single date that whole time."

"I've been busy."

Grace rolls her eyes. "And that's why you need my help. And here it is, in the form of a date with Noah Steel."

"But what do I *say* to him?"

"You talk about the kinds of stuff people normally talk about on dates. Like your hobbies. Your work—"

"I'm definitely not talking about my work. And I don't have hobbies."

She gives me an exasperated look. "You do have hobbies. You like to decorate your house. You like antiquing. You read sometimes, especially decorating magazines. You go to the movies occasionally. Every now and then you go to a museum or a play or a Broadway show. We saw Wicked for the third time just a few weeks ago. Tell him about that."

"Those aren't hobbies. Those are just…being alive and living in New York."

"Stop being so difficult, Lucky. Talk about your *favorite* book, your *favorite* movie, your *favorite* artist. Just let the conversation flow naturally."

Suddenly, the thought of sitting at a table with a total stranger and forcing small talk sounds terrifying, especially considering all the craziness going on in my life right now.

But Grace is right. It's one date.

"Just relax and enjoy it," Grace says encouragingly. "And who knows? Maybe this one date will lead to something amazing. Or not. But you'll never know either way until you at least try."

I sigh, feeling my resistance start to crumble. She's not wrong. A few hours of escape from my spiraling thoughts does sound sort of nice. And if he looks anything like he does in his photo, it might not be awful to stare at him for an hour or two before I take my leave.

"You can do this, Luck. Just put all the other stuff to the side for one evening and be in the moment. It's doable. You've got this."

I've got this? "What do I wear?"

She thinks about this for a few seconds, then her eyes light up. "That little blue dress you wore to that Heights exhibition we went to a few months ago. It's sexy as fuck."

"Do I…*want* to look sexy? God, I'm so bad at this."

"It's because you don't do it enough, sweetie. And yes,

you absolutely do want to look sexy." Grace asks gently, "So does this mean you're ready to accept the date?"

I'm nervous. "Do you really think I should?"

"I *really* think you should, Lucky Irish."

"Really?"

"*Yes.*"

I take a deep breath. "Okay. What the hell. Let's do this."

I'm still holding Grace's phone, which has gone dark. She guides my hand, bringing up the screen with the accept button. "You have to push the button. I'm not doing it for you."

"Here goes nothing." I do it. I click *Accept Your Date with Noah Steel.*

The screen flashes with digital confetti and fireworks. Then an address, the time and the date pops up, along with Noah Steel's face in a little polaroid with hearts popping around it.

Butterflies erupt in my stomach at the confirmation that this is actually happening, but Grace tops up our champagne. "This will be *so* good for you, Lucky, you'll see. Remember how it works. If you *pretend* you're about to meet the man of your absolute dreams, it just might turn out that you actually do."

9

NOAH

"If I didn't know better I'd say you were obsessed."

I glance up from my phone to see Colton leaning against my office doorway, trademark smirk in place. I set my phone on my desk, screen side down. But the damage is done. He's already caught me staring at Lucky Irish's photo.

Again.

I ended up downloading the app and getting Colton to log me in, so I could receive messages in case her plans changed. Or at least that's what I told him. The real reason I wanted the app on my phone is so I could study her sublime little sunshine-y face when no one was around. She's just so unbelievably fucking *cute*. I didn't know a person could *be* so flawless. "Just doing some final research before I embark on this date you forced on me," I bluff.

"Research, huh? Is that what the kids call stalking these days?"

I throw a pen at him, which he deftly catches. "Don't overthink it, bro."

"I'm not overthinking it." Even though I am. I've looked up every social media account associated with every variation of her name, but of course nothing has come up. This one photo and her fake name are all I have. It's hardly enough to justify my all-consuming fascination. I've hardly managed to get any work done at all. "What do you want, Cole? Don't you have work you're supposed to be doing?"

"Don't you?" More smirking, as he wanders into my office. "How many hours to go?"

Four hours and twenty minutes. "I don't know. A few."

He laughs. "I thought you might need a pre-date pep talk."

"From you? No thanks."

He ignores this. "The trick is to relax and play it cool."

"Ground-breaking advice from Casanova."

"Stop being such a grumpy fucker. You'll scare her away. What happened to the always-charming Noah Maddox?"

"Don't you mean Noah Steel?"

This reminder amuses him even more. "Dude, she's a girl, not an SEC watchdog. You shouldn't be this stressed out."

I lean back and fold my arms. "I'm not 'stressed out'."

"You are. You're getting all worked up because you're so out of practice. You're worried she's not as perfect in real life as she looks in her photo and that you'll be disappointed like you always are and that you'll have to let her down gently, which you don't want to have to do again because they always get immediately clingy once they find out about the bank balance—and also you're hot so they basically fall in love instantly and then you have to break their hearts," Colton rambles in one long breath.

I glare at him. He's not wrong. In fact he's hit the nail directly on the head. "Did you just call me hot?"

"Objectively speaking, I can recognize that you're not a complete troll, brother."

"Thanks. That means a lot, coming from you." He's making an attempt to help me relax and I can at least try to appreciate that.

"No more obsessing. You need to go in with zero expectations. Give me your phone."

I look down at it. "No." I don't want him deleting her photo.

"I'm not going to delete anything."

Colton takes my phone before I can grab it. "There." He hands it back to me.

"What did you do?"

"I logged you out. And I'm not telling you the password."

"Why? What the hell, Colton? What if she cancels?"

"She's not going to cancel. And you need to chill," he says firmly. "No more obsessing over her profile. Just meet the girl first and see if you vibe without any preconceived expectations."

I want to argue, but he's right—again—and it annoys me. "You're enjoying this way too much."

The smirk is back. "Consider it payback for all the unsolicited advice you've insisted on giving me over the years. Now go home and get ready for your date. Wear something sophisticated and dashing." Colton winks at me and laughs.

Before I can either punch him or tell him to fuck off, he's out the door, leaving me alone with my jumble of anticipation—and now without any outlet for my fanatical over-analyzation. Damn him.

With Colton gone, I try to focus on work, but my thoughts keep drifting back to Lucky Irish.

Those blue-on-blue eyes.

That white-gold hair with its jaunty little sun-lit curls.

Those lush pink lips, shiny with lip gloss. Lightly parted.

For me. For my—

Fuck.

Just the thought of her is me getting hard.

That saucy little phantom image of her feels like it's been seared into my brain by a sadistic blowtorch artist. I literally can't think of anything else. There's no point staying at the office. I need to head home, take a long, cold shower and pour myself a strong drink.

Avoiding everyone as I leave so I don't have to be on the receiving end of any more gleeful speculations, I take the back staircase.

I end up daydreaming as I weave my Ducati through the Friday afternoon traffic.

Will she really look as beautiful as she does in the photo?

Most likely not. How could she? No one's *that* perfect.

I need to prepare myself for disappointment. Most likely it'll happen the way it always does. She'll have photoshopped the image. She'll show up looking like a second-rate version of the original. She'll be perfectly nice but completely…ordinary, like they all are. We'll make polite conversation but there will be no fireworks, like I'm always hoping for but can never find. She'll talk about her Instagram following. Or her therapist. Or her cat. She'll flirt awkwardly and pretend she's not already picturing moving into my Hamptons house or going on wild shopping sprees with my money so she can make her vapid friends jealous by posting photos of herself living the high life.

Damn it.

Colton's right. I need to chill the fuck out.

It occurs to me though that, this time, my date doesn't know who I am. She'll have no idea about the money, the business or the family legacy.

I'm a totally blank slate to her.

I can make it up as I go along.

I can pretend, for a few hours, to be whoever the fuck I want.

So what if she's not the love of my life? It doesn't matter. None of them ever are.

So what if I don't fall in love with her at first sight? Obviously, I won't. Because that just doesn't happen to me. It might *never* happen.

I remember again my new resolution. To jump into bed at my very first opportunity without caring about the chemistry, just to get some of this pent-up frustration out of my goddamn system.

Watch out, Lucky Irish.

10

NOAH

IT ALMOST MAKES ME LAUGH. Lucky Irish. It's even worse than Noah Steel.

By the time I get back to my apartment I've almost succeeded in psyching myself up for a night of dirty deeds done dirt cheap with no emotion involved whatsoever. If worse comes to worst I'll close my eyes and *pretend* Lucky Irish is just as beautiful as the enchanting girl in the photo.

My apartment lights turn on as soon as I walk in. Low back-lighting that gives the place a luxurious ambiance. The steel-framed glass wall that looks out over Fifth Avenue shows off the late afternoon city skyline, my spacious outdoor roof garden and the treetops of Central Park.

I bought this apartment when things began to go stratospheric for us, a few years ago now. I paid twenty-five million for it. It's now worth forty.

I'm probably the most frugal of all four of us, but real estate is one thing I do spend money on. Actually, I don't skimp on cars or boats either. I have seven houses and I use all of them.

This penthouse is where I spend most of my time, but I also have a saltbox "cottage" in Southampton, a beach bungalow in the Bahamas, a waterfront villa on Lake Como, a small ranch with a house on the water in Austin, a mansion in the Hollywood Hills, and a beach house on the North Shore of Oahu. All the houses have several garages with a collection of cars, boats, jet skis and motorcycles that fit the driving and sailing conditions of the places they're in and are fun to take for joyrides.

New York City is in my veins and I've lived here my entire life. But if I don't get out of the city every now and then I feel like my sanity is starting to crack.

It was actually my idea to offer employees of Invested Enterprises a "creative" week each month. One week out of four, people can travel on the company. This way, we're encouraging our staff to come up with the kinds of new, innovative ideas you tend to get when you're visiting places you've always wanted to see and meeting people who challenge your own personal status quo.

We organize meetings with key people when we can, but not always. Sometimes they're free to just explore.

It's paid off. Almost forty percent of our new clients have been discovered and wooed that way. We're also the most sought-after company to work for in New York City, partly because of that one perk—even though we offer a lot of perks.

I work a lot, but I also do my best to use all my houses as much as I can on these weeks away. All my properties are very different. Each of them has such a different architectural style, and the backdrops and the culture of the places have so many different things to offer, they refresh me in new ways each time I visit.

But it's the same old story. I travel alone. If I take a woman to any one of my houses—including this one, and especially this one—she's begging me to put a ring on her finger within the hour. They get needy and desperate and want more than I ever want to give them.

And my problem is, I *do* want to give. I want to fucking *drown* in how in love I am for the one perfect girl I can never, ever find.

Which brings me back to my plans for the evening.

To forget about my spiritual cravings and focus instead on my feral *animal* cravings.

I pour myself two fingers of whiskey and knock back the whole thing. Then I go out to my pool, strip down and dive in. No one can see me up here. The privacy is a big part of why this apartment was so pricey, but it's worth it. As a Maddox, we tend to get a certain amount of attention. Not something I aspire to at all. None of us do, except maybe Colton. He's the only one of us who really enjoys the publicity.

I do fifty laps. Then I grab a towel and go inside to take a long shower.

None of it takes the edge off.

I put on jeans, a nice shirt and my leather jacket.

I still have an hour. Since it's only a few blocks to the restaurant, I decide to walk. Maybe a stroll down Fifth Avenue will do me good.

It's Friday evening and everything's busy. There's a festive spark in the air and I feel that bubble of glittering anticipation kick up my heartbeat. I'm trying hard *not* to think about how beautiful Lucky Irish's photo was. Or to get my hopes up. Or to fixate on the fact that *she can't actually look like that.*

Without even thinking about it, as I walk past Tiffany's, I go inside.

I don't know why.

I don't know what I'm looking for.

But then I see it.

Our mother used to wear a diamond tennis bracelet. All the time. She even slept in it. Looking back on it and knowing what I now know about diamonds, my father would have easily paid several million dollars for that bracelet. Its jewels sparkled even in the dark.

It's a vague memory but I remember asking her once —I was maybe six or seven years old at the time—if she'd ever taken it off. She smiled and touched my hair. My mother used to love my hair. It was blond when I was young. *Angel's curls*, she used to call it. *I never take it off, darling,* she told me, *because it's my magic bracelet. It keeps me safe and it makes me happy.* My mother had grown up poor and married my father when she was very young. I never really thought about the details of her past when I was a kid but I remember being charmed at the time by the thought of her magic bracelet.

She was buried with the bracelet still on.

The one I'm looking at now is made of sapphires.

They're exactly the same color as Lucky Irish's eyes. Again, I remind myself that the color was probably photoshopped in.

I don't know why I do it. "I'll take it," I tell the woman behind the counter.

"Of course, sir." She doesn't miss a beat. "Will that be cash or card?"

I slide my black credit card across the glass.

A very swish team of personnel have the card swiped and the bracelet wrapped into its blue box with a white ribbon before I can change my mind.

I slide the wrapped box into my jacket pocket. "Thank you." I leave the store not actually knowing how much money I just spent. I'm a fucking CFO, I *always* know how much money I've spent.

Maybe I'm going crazy. This monumental dry spell is messing with my head.

Of course I'm not going to give it to her. She's a stranger. I just…want to have it in my pocket. In case.

In case of what, you asshole? You just can't let it go, can you?

You refuse to stop hoping that this girl will be The One. It's always your fatal mistake. Hoping too hard.

Anyway.

It's just off dusk. I get to the restaurant ten minutes early. It's a new place I haven't been to before. It has brick walls, wooden beams, a few leather couches and a lot of lamps. I guess it is romantic. It's tastefully decorated. Raised booths with tables line the walls and give a certain amount of privacy to each one. There's a hotel desk at one end of the dining room and gold-plated elevator doors. Colton mentioned there's a new five-star hotel upstairs.

The maître d' approaches me. "Table for one, sir?"

"Two. I'm not sure if I have a reservation or not. My name is Noah M—uh, Steel. Noah Steel." Fucking Colton. Then again, I'm glad. If Lucky Irish and I don't hit it off, she has no way of finding out who I am.

It doesn't matter if you hit it off or not. You made a decision. You're not looking for love. All you're looking for is someone compatible enough to have a good time with for one night and one night only. It's time to let off some much-needed steam, Noah Steel. This is your opportunity. Make the most of it.

"Right this way, Mr. Steel. You've got the best table in the house."

I follow him to the front table, which is up three stairs in its own private booth but also next to the window with a view of the door. A small table lamp is on, casting a golden glow.

He sets the menus on the table. "I'll show Ms. Irish to her seat as soon as she arrives. Our Lucky in Love customers have really been hitting it off. I hope you enjoy your night, Mr. Ma—uh, Mr. Steel."

I'm not exactly thrilled that the dating app makes the reservation. And it's obvious this guy recognizes me, which isn't unusual in this neighborhood. I've been on the cover of Forbes twice and our company gets written up all the time. I can only hope Lucky Irish travels in different circles. *If you say so, buddy.* "Thanks."

Once he's gone I check my watch. 7:05.

A waitress brings two glasses of water. "Can I get you a drink, Mr. Steel?"

"We'd like a bottle of Moët on ice." Might as well get the ball rolling.

She winks at me. "Of course. Coming right up."

She leaves and I have nothing left to do but wait, checking my watch every thirty seconds.

What if she doesn't show up?

Is she nervous? Scared? Is she okay?

A flash of golden blond glides past the window below me.

It's her.

She's wearing a blue dress that's one shade lighter than Lucky Irish's eyes in the photo.

And the sapphires in my pocket.

She stands in the doorway for a few seconds, like she's thinking twice about coming in.

Even from this distance, I can see that the photo hardly did her justice. She's cute but also gorgeous. Her eyes are blue even from across the room. The bright colors of her hair, her dress and the pink bag she's carrying are eye-catching on their own, but it's her face that has me riveted.

I'm quite literally starstruck. My mouth feels parched. And my heart aches as though I've been missing something monumental and here it suddenly fucking is.

Holy fuck.

She's so *beautiful.*

The maître d' approaches her and she introduces herself. He points toward our booth and they both glance in my direction. At that moment, her eyes meet mine.

11

———

One hour earlier

"STOP FIDGETING AND HOLD STILL."

Grace insisted on glamming me up for my date. It's been a very long time since I glammed up *this* much. In fact, I can't remember *ever* glamming up this much. "It's just a first date, Gracie. I'm not running off to Vegas with him."

"Ninety-eight percent compatibility is no joke, Luck. He could be the *one*. We need to prepare you for that." Grace applies more glossing product to my hair.

"Just because you got lucky doesn't mean I will."

"That's not the attitude we need right now, girlfriend. If Lucky *Irish* can't get lucky then we're all doomed."

"He might not even show up. Then all your efforts will be wasted."

"Oh, he'll show," Grace says. "He's not going to stand up his perfect match. And then when he takes one look at you, he'll have no choice but to fall head over heels in love with you. Not that you're not gorgeous in your corporate power suits *or* your sweatpants, but damn, girl, you should do this more often." She stands back from my hair and make-up, surveying her work. "I'm a genius. And you, my friend, are *stunning*. Noah Steel won't stand a chance."

I look in the mirror at my perfectly defined waves that now frame my unusually-glamorous face. I look…good. Maybe better than I've ever looked.

I'm generally a keep-it-natural kind of girl, which Grace gets, but she's definitely taken things to the next level. The smoky eyes are sexy, my cheeks look smooth but my sprinkling of freckles still shines through. My lips look full and glossy, a shade somewhere between hot pink and Taylor Swift red.

"Okay, I concede you might know what you're doing. I look like I'm almost worthy of a private box at a Chiefs game."

"I told you a make-over wasn't a terrible idea. Okay, go put on your dress. You've only got half an hour until your Uber gets here. I booked one for you so you can't change your mind."

My stomach does a funny little flip.

We've already decided on my dress. It happens to be one of my favorites. The few times I've worn it I've always gotten compliments.

As I go into my room to put it on, Grace calls after me, "And make sure you wear those lacy white panties and matching wonder bra." We happened to be downtown the other day and bought a few things at Victoria's Secret.

"Yes, boss. But don't get your hopes up."

"Oh, my hopes are way, *way* up, bestie."

I laugh, but then it sinks in what she's actually referring to and the thought causes those butterflies in my stomach to once again erupt into flight. *Getting laid by Noah Steel.*

Yeah, right.

Sure, Grace got totally swept away, but I'm not Grace. I'm hardly going to jump into bed with a total stranger on our first date.

When it comes to dating, I'm extremely cautious. Obviously, since I'm a twenty-three-year-old virgin who's never been in a serious relationship in my life.

I've agreed to this date only because Grace talked me into it, but the chances of tonight leading to a second date are slim. I don't care what the app said. How can an algorithm know anything about chemistry anyway? I'll grin and bear the next few hours in the interest on trying to break out of my hermit-like existence, forget my many threatening-to-overflow troubles and enjoy a night out on the town for a change.

I dutifully follow Grace's instructions, putting on the sexy undies and the tight-fitting dress, which hangs just past the top of my thighs. I carefully loop my gold pendant necklace over my head, so I don't mess up my hair. I wear this pendant every day. At the end of it hangs a gold four-leaf clover charm that used to be my mother's. I put on matching gold hoop earrings and pull on a pair of gold strappy heels.

I stare at myself in the mirror for a few seconds. The image could be my mother staring back at me. I look so much like her when she was my age, in the photo of her when she'd just arrived in New York, it's almost eerie.

I've never really thought of myself as beautiful. Cute, maybe. My mother was stunning. But now that I take a moment to consider it, this new, glammed up vision of myself…I *do* look beautiful. I don't have that many people in my life who point that out to me very often. Grace, yes. But we're busy people. My father, no. He was too distracted. And he avoided looking at me because I reminded him too much of her.

I wish you were here, Mama.

I wish we could have had more time together.

I wish I wasn't so alone.

I wish I wasn't staring down the barrel of bankruptcy, destitu-tion and/or homelessness.

Anyway.

Tonight isn't about my woes. It's about my hot date with Noah Steel, who I'm very hopeful is neither a troll nor a psycho killer. We'll have a drink or two. We'll laugh about how we have nothing in common and the app was all wrong. We'll say goodnight and I'll pick up exactly where I left off.

I grab my pink Chanel bag—another of my mother's splurges. It matched the pink suit that still hangs at the back of my closet. I don't wear the suit but I use the bag on special occasions and I'm pretending this qualifies. I walk back to the kitchen.

Grace has put on a dress for her own date. It's green silk and very slinky. Her jaw drops when I walk out of my room. "Holy shit, Luck. You look *gorgeous*."

"So do you, Gracie. That dress is hot, girl. It's giving sultry mermaid."

"Exactly what I was going for." She hands me one of two glasses of wine she just poured. "That eyeshadow is just…" She mimes a chef's kiss motion. "Look out, Noah Steel. Your life is about to change."

"I still don't know how I'm supposed to take him seriously with a name that sounds like it's straight out of a spy thriller."

"Or an erotic romance novel," she smirks, clinking her glass against mine. "To getting laid tonight."

"As if," I laugh, shaking my head. I take a sip of wine, the liquid courage warming me from the inside out. But not too much. I need my wits.

My phone dings from inside my bag.

"That must your ride."

"Either that or Noah Steel is canceling." Grace finally

allowed me to download the dating app. But it's not a message from Noah Steel. It's the Uber. "I better go."

"Wait." She takes my phone.

"What are you doing?"

"Turning on your Snap Map. For safety reasons."

"In case he *does* turn out to be a psycho killer?"

"In case he takes you to his apartment after your date," she clarifies. "For the getting laid part of the evening."

"Would you stop?"

Grace gives me a hug. "Have fun, and give Noah Steel a real chance, even if his name sounds like he should be fighting supervillains instead of right-swiping."

"You have a good night too, bestie. Say hi to Ethan for me."

"Maybe we can double date next time."

"Yeah. Sure," I scoff.

"Good luck, sweetie."

"Thanks. I'll need it."

12

Lucky

I TAKE THE ELEVATOR DOWN. My Uber is waiting at the curb.

The driver has music playing. He doesn't try to make conversation and I'm glad. I need a minute.

The city is busy tonight. A man in a suit on the street talking on his phone as he walks reminds me of my disastrous phone call with Cash Maddox. His veiled threats about my financial situation. His offer that happens to be five million dollars short of what I need to survive, but that I might be forced to accept anyway or face bankruptcy.

Asshole.

But it's not Cash Maddox's fault that I'm in this mess. I'm probably going to face bankruptcy no matter what happens.

Unless his evil CFO agrees to my price, of course. Which somehow seems unlikely. The guy sounds like a piece of work.

But what if his CFO *did* agree to it?

Cash was willing to pay more. The CFO is his brother, surely Cash can persuade him.

What if they offer me the price I want?

What would I do then?

Accept it, of course.

And then what?

If I'm free to make any choice I want, what would I choose to do next?

It's a good question. One I haven't really allowed myself to think about very often, because I've always known I would take over my father's business. From day one. It was implied in every conversation we ever had. It went hand in hand with being the only Ashton heir—and with living in the Ashton residence, which is all I ever really cared about.

Looking back on it now, I should have stood up for myself a little bit more. I should have thought more about what *I* actually *wanted.*

What do I want?

What would I do if I could do anything at all in the whole wide world?

Deep down, I know exactly what I'd do.

It's almost embarrassing to admit to myself. My

deeply-buried ideal life probably doesn't sound modern or progressive or aspirational at all to a lot of people. But to me it's the most aspirational life of all.

In my heart, what I really want to do is to have a whole bunch of babies and lavish my attention on them like my mother used to do to me, before our time together was cut so short.

She *loved* being a mother. She loved being *my* mother.

It's what I want too, more than anything. In this day and age it almost sounds archaic. I genuinely respect the hell out of all the hard work feminists have done throughout the decades and I don't mean to seem ungrateful. Of course I'm grateful I'm a CEO—and not a terrible one, even though I've inherited a terrible situation. I'm incredibly lucky to be where I am and to have all the opportunities I've had, especially since I'm young. I know that and I appreciate it.

But finance and investing have never been my passions. I'm good at reading spreadsheets because it's the only thing my father and I ever bonded over. It's the only thing we ever had in common, except for the sorrow of losing the one person we both loved most of all.

If it was up to me, I'd happily never look at a goddamn spreadsheet again in my life.

If I could live *any* life I wanted to…I'd get married to some charming, twinkly-eyed man who makes me laugh. Maybe even an Irish one. I'd have babies and I'd create a beautiful, loving home.

I can't think of a single thing I don't covet about the idea of it. I'd cook organic baby food and create the most nurturing environment to raise them in. I'd love those babies so much it almost hurts to think about.

Maybe I'd start a small interior design business on the side. Maybe I could capitalize on my knack for making my living spaces comfortable and cozy, but in a stylish way. Everyone who visits my apartment comments on it. People have asked me if I hire out my time or if I've thought about starting an influencer account. I've always said no, because I was always too busy studying and working.

It's strange. This is actually the first time I've ever admitted to myself that I want a family more than anything else. Not a high-powered finance career. Not a flailing company that was someone else's obsession, but never mine.

Either way, my dream will have to wait. Bankruptcy isn't exactly the ideal foundation for the stable, happy home I want to give my future babies—*if* they're meant to be, at some point in an uncertain, distant future.

Besides, you need a man for babies.

Or a sperm donor.

Or a spur-of-the-moment trip to Ireland, to have a one-night stand with a sparkly-eyed charmer with tousled hair who smells like fresh air and green grass.

Jesus. I need to calm down. Stress is spinning my

thoughts in weird directions. My fantasies could be straight out of an Irish Spring commercial.

Get a grip, girl.

But it does remind me that I haven't been back to Ireland since before my mother died. This suddenly feels like a huge oversight. I was only three years old when we went to meet my grandparents, who have since passed away, and my mother's many cousins. One thing I do remember is that my mother was so, so happy.

The Uber slows to a stop.

Shit. We're here.

"Here you are, Miss Irish. I hope the date goes well."

"Oh. Thanks." Grace must have used my dating app alibi.

I can see the sign for Hopeless Romantic two doors down.

The Uber pulls away and I stand on the sidewalk for a few seconds, wondering if I actually want to go through with this. Honestly, despite the Irish Spring commercial, the last thing I want to do right now is to make small talk with some random guy from the internet. This whole thing feels like a mistake waiting to happen.

No doubt "Noah Steel" will turn out to be totally underwhelming compared to his picture. He's probably some middle manager from New Jersey. Not that there's anything *wrong* with middle managers from New Jersey, but the vision doesn't really mesh with my Irish Spring fantasies.

Even if Noah Steel is half as attractive as his online picture, I'm not really in the mood for this. I'm stressed out and exhausted. I don't know how Grace managed to talk me into it.

Part of me is very tempted to keep walking right past the restaurant and blow off this joke of a date. But Grace will murder me if I don't at least meet him.

With a resigned sigh, I head toward the door.

Inside, the place is cute and nicely decorated. It's busy.

The host greets me with a smile. "Welcome to Hopeless Romantic. Do you have a reservation?"

"Uh, yes. Under Lucky Irish." I feel foolish even saying it.

But the host is excited. "Miss Irish! Welcome. Mr. Steel is already here. Please, follow me."

God. My heart is beating like crazy.

Grace, I'm going to kill you for this.

I follow the host across the room, and I see a man stand up from his seat at a raised corner table. In the romantically-lit space, it's already clear that Noah Steel is definitely as good-looking as his photo. Or even more so.

Much, much more so. Because he's real.

He's big. Taller than I was expecting. And *built*, I can't help but notice.

He's wearing a white button-down shirt with the top few buttons undone, showing off that same tanned, corded neck I was staring at through my phone only a few hours ago. The white of his shirt highlights the warmth of his cinnamon skin.

He looks almost out of place, like he's not a New Yorker at all, but a rodeo hero from out west, somewhere with big skies and long, lazy days of summer sun.

I don't know why I say that. He just looks…*hotter* than any New Yorker I've ever seen. Too beefed-up and healthy for a city-dweller.

His eyes, as I get closer—and my heart feels like it's about to beat its way right out of my chest—are that same sky blue that they were in his photo. They're fixed on me intently. Sliding lower. To my dress and all the many details its tight fit and short skirt reveals, before traveling back up to my face. His gaze on my body makes me feel…*warm.*

Help.

His hair is a rich shade of brown with tints of red from the many golden lights in the room.

Holy hell, he's gorgeous.

It's the kind of over-the-top handsomeness that could almost be intimidating. *This Adonis is my actual date?* Why would someone like this need a dating app?

But then he smiles, and it's so genuine that I can't help kind of relaxing into this. Those little crinkles around his eyes and his killer, endearing smile are outra-geously…attractive. And inviting. My very first impression —aside from that he's hot AF—is that he's trustworthy. "You must be Lucky. I'm Noah. It's nice to meet you."

His voice is smooth and deep with a lightly smoky rasp at the edges that causes the tiny hairs on my body rise. "You too," I manage.

He offers me his hand. As I watch his eyes, I take it. It's big and warm and almost unnervingly strong. He squeezes my hand and the light pressure sends a channel of molten awareness through my entire body. There's a warm, fluttery pulse *inside* me that's…*oh my god.*

His broad shoulders and muscular arms fill out his shirt to the point where it's almost straining the thick cotton fabric.

Jesus. He must work out a lot.

He releases my hand and offers me a seat. "After you, Lucky Irish."

I laugh lightly at our ridiculous names. "Thank you, Noah Steel."

We sit in the cozy leather booth with its view of the restaurant and the street out the window down below us that I can only vaguely appreciate because I can barely pull my gaze away from my date enough to take it all in. But the place's name fits. It *feels* romantic. And I'm suddenly very glad I didn't keep walking.

"I hope you like champagne." He takes the bottle out of an ice bucket that's propped next to the table. "I took the liberty of ordering for us. Or we can order you something else if you prefer."

"I like champagne." I blink up at him. I'm kind of mesmerized by the color of his eyes. They could almost be described as duck-egg blue, with little shards of gold and darker blues, like rare, stolen jewels.

Noah Steel's smile holds and it's so beguiled, I'd almost say he's as spellbound as I am. With a hot edge behind his blue gaze, still holding mine, my insides feel like they've turned into a molten, lava-like liquid that's warming me with sublime…anticipation, maybe.

And with awe. Those almost-red tints in his hair and the little flicks of it behind his ears are charming me. If he's a corporate type, he's a little overdue for a haircut. It's got a barely-there wave to it and it's not quite but almost…tousled.

I wonder what he'd look like without that expensive-looking shirt on, in an outdoor shower in the countryside, those muscles all soaped up.

Would you stop with the Irish Spring commercial already?

But he could: he absolutely could have stepped straight out of one.

That warm, fluttery pulse in a *very* intimate place is gaining momentum. *Oh my god, my panties are getting wet.*

I've actually never in my life had dirty thoughts about a man, especially not one that's real. But Noah Steel is just so freaking gorgeous, my body is reacting to him in crazy ways.

"So, are you actually Irish?" he drawls, pouring two glasses of champagne and handing me one.

"Yes. My mother was an O'Callahan from County

Cork." *Why did I tell him that?* I'm giving away real info and we're supposed to be playing our roles here.

"My mother's father was a Sullivan from Dublin." He clinks his glass against mine.

Oh shit. The sincere smile and the blue eyes and the hair and the muscles *and* he's got Irish in him?

This is a man I could fall in love with.

13

———

NOAH

Lucky Irish approaches the table and I stand up, wondering if my eyes are playing tricks on me.

Am I hallucinating? Have I stepped into some alternate universe where all my wildest dreams are suddenly realized? Because I can only stare with beguiled fascination at the girl walking toward me.

She's blond, but it's not a typical blond. It's not ash or sandy or bleach-blond, but a bright honey gold that's streaked with platinum. It's wavy, hanging to barely touch her shoulders, with those same whimsical, jaunty curls as in her photo.

I don't usually stop to think about how "natural" a woman is. I don't care how much she spends at the hairdresser or what she does to enhance herself at whatever kind of spas or salons women go to these days. But what I notice about Lucky Irish is that she's very noticeably *like this*, without even trying to be. It's not a manufactured beauty, but one that's unapologetically real. Amazingly, she seems completely unaware of how gorgeous she is.

With her clear blue eyes, her flawless skin and a playful sprinkling of freckles across the bridge of her nose, she's young and fresh-looking, like she just walked out of a dewy garden on a sunny spring morning. You half expect bluebirds and butterflies to flutter around her.

She's slim but also lusciously curvy in all the right places.

Fucking hell.

That blue dress leaves almost nothing to the imagination—and my imagination is on overdrive.

Does she look this way to everyone? Why isn't every man in New York chasing after her right now? How can anyone be so insanely drop-dead gorgeous?

I can only pray to the Lord Almighty that it's not obvious I'm already revved into high gear. My cock has *not* been happy with my monk-like choices lately and, as much as I'm trying to remain calm, it's refusing to cooperate. *I'm hard as a fucking rock.* Which isn't the easiest thing to hide when you happen to be…me. My jacket—thank fuck—hides the worst of it.

She's close now and I can read that she's nervous, even as she holds my gaze. So I smile, partly to ease her nerves and partly because I can't help it. She's far more beautiful than her photo. This makes me wildly happy.

"You must be Lucky." *And I must be even luckier.* I hold out my hand. "I'm Noah. It's nice to meet you."

Jesus, how am I supposed to play it cool when she looks like *this*?

"You too." The breathlessness of her softly-spoken reply is almost more than I can handle. I don't know why. The light husk of her voice makes me feel like I've morphed into a yeti who will protect this feminine softness of her with my life. It's intense to suddenly *feel* so much, and with so little warning. A flood of *want* is pumping through my veins with so much force, I feel a weird kind of vertigo.

Here she is. I finally found her.

I ignore the crazy talk going on in my brain right now and focus instead on Lucky Irish's face, which is dazzling me like nothing ever has. I offer her a seat. "After you, Lucky Irish."

Her giggle at the fake name she's given herself sends more blood south and, with less of it in my brain, my new obsession is making me almost dizzy with it. "Thank you, Noah Steel."

At this point, the description isn't wrong. "I hope you like champagne. Or we can order something else if you prefer."

"I like champagne." She blinks at me and—*holy fuck.* Is it possible to fall in love at first sight? Because I think it might be happening to me in slow motion. I think I might already be a hundred percent besotted with this fresh-faced, golden-haired little nymph. She's so *beautiful*. On purely a physical level, she's so…*what I want*. Her perfection is messing with my head.

She sits and I sit next to her but not too close. There's no telling what I might do.

I pour the champagne, trying not to stare. "So, are you actually Irish?"

"Yes. My mother was an O'Callahan from County Cork."

There's a light nostalgia in her voice when she mentions her mother. I can't help but notice the *was*. Not *is*. Something we have in common, then. And a topic I'll save for later. She bites her lip, like she's wondering if she's confessed too much already. So I give her the same level of honesty. "My mother's father was a Sullivan from Dublin."

Something about this information digs into Lucky Irish, I can tell. She likes it. Her eyes get even more blue, if that's possible.

"So, did you come up with the name Lucky Irish yourself?"

She laughs. "No. That was my best friend Grace's idea. She created my profile on that dating app. I haven't been on a date in…a while. She thought I needed to get out more." Her eyes are still on mine. Like mine are on hers. "How about you, Noah Steel?"

I laugh, running my hand across my jaw. "That name was my brother's idea. So was the dating app. He thinks I work too much. He thinks I need to loosen up and socialize more. He'd heard of the app and signed me up."

"So we're both here against our will."

I clink my glass against hers. "To being here against our will." I can't help myself. "And to our Irish luck. And the most beautiful blind date I could have imagined." It sounds cheesy but I don't fucking care. She deserves all the praise I can give her.

Lucky smiles and it's so cute-hot, my chest feels tight with longing. For what, I'm not sure. Okay, I'm sure. For her. *To kiss those lush lips and get my first taste.* "Where are you from?"

"Born and bred right here in the Big Apple."

"How about that." Her smile lingers. "So am I."

"So now we know two things about each other. And they both match."

"I guess at ninety-eight point two percent, we're bound to have a few things in common." She takes a sip of her champagne as she continues to watch me.

"I guess we are." *Wow, she's gorgeous.* "Tell me more. What does Lucky Irish do when she's not being set up on blind dates with random strangers? The app mentioned you work in finance."

As if she weren't perfect enough, little dimples tweak playfully. "Yes."

"So do I."

"How about that." She touches her tongue to her plump bottom lip, causing my hard-on to crank up at least one more notch. "Another thing we have in common."

My voice sounds low and husky as I dig deeper. I know it might strike a nerve as I ask it, but I want to know more about her. *I want to know if she's okay. If she's safe.* My curiosity is almost manic. I need to calm the fuck down. "Is your family still in New York?" If I didn't know better, she could be in her late teens, she looks that young.

The playfulness fades out. "No. Both my parents died. I'm an only child. I live with the same best friend who set me up on this date."

"Grace."

"Yes. Grace."

"I'm sorry to hear about your parents. I lost mine too."

"You did? When?"

"My mother died when I was seven. My dad had a heart attack around four years ago."

She watches me for a few seconds. "I was four when my mother died. My dad died only recently."

"I'm sorry." She's alone and this feels strangely unbearable. Some new protective instinct flares and I have to fight the urge to reach out and weave my fingers through hers.

"So, I guess we're both orphans," she says.

"I never really thought of it that way but, yeah, I guess we are."

She exhales a light laugh at her own choice of words.

"It sounds very Oliver Twist, but the whole concept has kind of knocked me around recently."

"It's a hard thing to adjust to," I agree.

"You said you have a brother."

"Three, actually."

"Wow. Well, there's our one point eight percent point of difference." She's got a quirky little sense of humor that practically has me on my knees. "Are you close with them?"

"You could say that. They drive me crazy, but they're also my best friends. We lean on each other more than we'd like to admit."

"You're lucky to have them."

"I am. Even if they annoy me on practically an hourly basis."

She smiles quietly. There are big holes in her life I understand only too well. I *am* lucky that my brothers insist on filling the holes in my life whether I want them to or not.

"I'm sorry you've lost so much."

She shrugs a little. "I have Grace. She's like a sister. She lives with me. She met her new boyfriend through this same dating app, so she insisted I try it."

"Grace is quickly becoming one of my favorite people."

Lucky twirls a strand of her flaxen hair absentmindedly around her finger. "Is your name actually Noah?"

"Yes. What about yours? Give me your first name, at least."

"Lucky is my real name."

My eyes narrow. "Yeah?"

"It even says so on my birth certificate."

This charms me even more. "You look like a Lucky."

"And you look like a Noah."

I can't tell if she's teasing me. "Is that a good thing?"

"Yes. Noah's the kind of guy who will talk you off a ledge or save the day when things go wrong. Always dependable. Trustworthy. Almost always honorable. A borderline control freak."

I laugh. "You nailed it."

"What, then, are Noah Steel's wildest dreams?"

I'm not expecting the question and something about it spears me right in the chest. I don't think anyone has ever asked me that, point blank with blue, blue eyes. Coming from someone as knock-out stunning as Lucky Irish, it hits me where I live. "You want the honest answer?"

"Of course I do."

She wants honesty. I only hope it doesn't scare her away. But to hell with that. I'd already run after her. "To fall in love."

Her smile is beguiled, like I've caught her off guard. "Really?"

"Really."

"You're just saying that."

"I'm not. It's true. You can ask my brothers."

"That's very…*romantic* of you, Mr. Steel."

"Guilty as charged. I'm always getting accused of being a romantic. I'm not sure why though. Out of all four of us, I'm the only one who's still unattached."

"Maybe you were just waiting for the right person."

"Maybe I was." *And I've got the craziest feeling I've just found her.* "What are Lucky Irish's wildest dreams?"

She pauses, like she's not sure she wants to tell me. But then she says, "You know, it's funny, I've never really thought about it much because I've been busy with school or work, but I was actually thinking about that exact question on my way over here."

"And what did you decide?"

The light pinkness of her cheeks as she smiles is driving me slightly insane at this point. She's mind-numbingly lovely. "I can't tell you that."

"That's not fair. I told you mine."

"You'd laugh. It sounds weird, even to me."

I top up her champagne. "I promise I won't laugh."

She gives me a lightly sassy look and—*fucking hell*—my obsession digs deeper. *I love her face. I love the way her hair curls like it's got a mind of its own. I love those little dimples like I've morphed into an obsessed madman. I love her lush mouth.* "You promise?"

I set the bottle back into the ice bucket and place my hand over my heart. "I'm not going to laugh."

She still won't tell me.

"I can wait. Another thing about Noahs is that we're

patient," I tell her. "And very persistent. We've got all night, Irish."

There's the smile. She relents a little. "Well…the thing is, I've got kind of a high-powered job. Which I'm grateful for. But to be honest, it isn't really me at all."

"It isn't?"

"No."

"What *is* you, Lucky Irish?"

"All I really want to do is…" Eyeing me. "No. I can't."

"You said it yourself. Noahs are trustworthy, remember? Tell me. You have to now."

Her blue eyes rove over my face, lightly spellbound. I've never wanted to kiss anyone with this kind of voracious need before in my life. I can't help it. Slowly, I reach for her hand. Willing myself to take it as carefully as I'm capable of, I rub my thumb across her smooth palm.

Holy fuck. I'm touching her. She exists and she's perfect.

Lucky watches my hand, now wrapped around hers, but she doesn't pull away. "In a perfect world I'll fall madly in love. I'll become…enlightened about all the things that go along with falling in love. Things I haven't experienced yet. And then one day—not today, obviously —but one day, what I really want is to have a family. I know it might sound old-fashioned, but I didn't get to spend a lot of time with my own mother and I feel like I really missed out on that. I've missed her every single day. I still miss her every single day. I want to be able to spend all my time with my own babies. I want to have lots of them and just...*be* there for them. Cook for them. Decorate a beautiful home for us. And dedicate my time to my family. I would love to do that." She stops and a light blush warms her cheeks. "Crazy, right? Not exactly trendy in New York City."

It's a visceral reaction on a very deep, primal level. When she says the word *family*, my heart sort of breaks and beats more heavily, more purposefully. At the mention of the word *babies*, my cock thickens hotly, almost painfully. I can't explain any of it, but her reply slays me. It's ridiculously fast but all I can think about is that *I want it to be me.* "That's the best goddamn dream I've ever heard."

14

"I can't believe I just told you that."

"I'm glad you did."

He's so damn easy to talk to. Something about his manly fascination is crazily alluring. He's smart and perceptive and so *tuned in*, he feels like a long lost friend. A very masculine, *hot* best friend who also happens to be a good listener who's on exactly the same wavelength as me, like we're tuned into the same celestial frequency. He's so handsome it almost hurts to look at him directly. It's like staring into the sun.

It's a heady cocktail.

Not only that, but he's holding my hand.

Like, *really* holding it. Weaving his fingers through mine. Playing with it lightly. Touching me with a kind of awe.

His hands are so big. So warm. Strong. Barely rough.

"My aspirations are very 50's housewife," I joke, feeling self-conscious that I've admitted to the most gorgeous man I've ever seen that the thought of being barefoot and pregnant sounds downright dreamy to me. I mean, not *now*, obviously. But I don't want to wait forever, either. My mother had me when she was twenty-three. Because of that, the thought of starting young always appealed to me.

I've never even unveiled this little morsel of truth to Grace. And now this stranger knows more about me than my best friend.

In my defense, I honestly don't think I've ever *clicked* with someone so instantly before.

He asked the question into a perfect donut hole of inhibitions loosened by champagne and a spark-heavy atmosphere that, with him in it, inexplicably feels like one where dreams actually *could* come true. Noah Steel makes unicorns seem possible. I can't explain it, but there it is.

"I don't think you're the only one," he says. "Maybe it's the start of a cultural shift. An instinctual backlash to the way society has at least doubled the workload of women in the past few decades. I read somewhere that women who work full-time still do ninety-percent of the household chores and eighty-seven percent of the child-rearing. And they're working hours that are at least equal to men's and sometimes more. That sounds exhausting."

"Yeah. It does." I'm a little surprised by his comments. He's more evolved than the men I'm used to.

All the nerd dinosaurs at my father's company hate that I'm a woman *and* their CEO. I choose to ignore their outdated point of view, but I can read the vibes in the boardroom. They're still visualizing that glass ceiling, wishing like hell I hadn't put so many cracks in it.

"Plus," he continues, "women are still paid less than men, on average. Do you find that in your workplace?"

Damn, his eyes are blue. "No." I'm the CEO. I make sure I'm getting the same salary my father got. Unfortunately, it's still not enough to keep my boat from taking on some serious water.

When I don't elaborate, he says, "Tell me about your job."

I watch as his thumb glides along my palm, scratching lightly like a cat's tongue. This small roughness feeds little tendrils of warmth to that fluttery sensation *inside* me. *Yikes.* "I'm not talking about work with you, Mr. Steel."

His slow smile has a dark, playful edge. "All right. That would be giving me too much information and I haven't earned your trust yet. I get it. You'll be happy to know I have every intention of rising to your challenge."

"Is that right?" *God, my panties really are…wet.*

"Yes, it is, Ms. Irish. And since you did already tell me you're hoping to get knocked up at some point in the near future, I think my powers are working. My brothers always tell me I've got a knack for getting them to admit things that no one else can. We're off to a good start."

Heat rises to my face. *And in the low pit of my belly, where warmth continues to pool.* "I did not say I want to get 'knocked up'."

"Semantics, Irish."

"Now I'm regretting telling you."

"No, you're not," comes the smug drawl. "So, do you have a timeframe in mind? For the insemination?"

This makes me laugh. "Oh my god. I did not say it like that. I meant in the future—*distant* future, obviously."

"It's better not to wait too long if you want lots of them."

"Sage advice from Mr. Steel."

Noah blinks at me. There's empathy swirled through his teasing, and the combination, along with dark eyelashes that are far too long for a man's, makes me hate him a little. Because I already know he's going to be impossible to resist. "What does the whole scenario look like in your mind? Describe it to me."

And here he goes again with the gently coaxing questions that are asked with such interest and such care, you can't help but answer them. "I don't know. In my mind, it all just happens in a fairy tale of perfect timing, and then I'm surrounded by all these magical little beings who I get to take care of. And this time I get the whole happily ever after and not just the first part, which is all my mother ever got."

Again, I'm amazed at what I'm admitting to Noah. With him, it just feels easy to let it out. Behind his over-the-top masculinity, he has this aura of kindness that makes my heart hurt.

Turns out kindness and hotness are one hell of a combination.

"Is there going to be a man involved in all of this baby-making?" Gently, but there's a cockiness to it too, which I have no idea what to do with.

I don't mention my earlier thoughts about the sperm bank or a spur-of-the-moment trip to Ireland. "Maybe." *Am I teasing him?* "I mean, yes, of course, but I only need him for one tiny thing. There are options available these days."

"Okay." His low chuckle might almost offend me if it wasn't the sexiest thing I've ever heard.

What the hell are you even telling him all this for? You're losing your mind! Or at least your inhibitions. No more champagne for you, girlfriend.

I'm almost grateful for the interruption when the waiter arrives to tell us about the specials. Noah orders a steak and I order mushroom pasta. He orders another bottle of champagne, which is brought to us almost immediately.

I keep waiting for the red flags. My instincts are usually pretty good. But with Noah Steel, so far it's a sea of green. Which is borderline unnerving. Especially when he's *this* freaking gorgeous.

What's he hiding? What secrets will emerge to bite me in the ass? There has to be a catch. No one's this perfect.

"If I'm not allowed to ask you about work," he says, "tell me something else about yourself. Where do you live? Generally speaking, I mean. I'm not asking for an exact address."

I guess that's safe enough. "I've lived in the same apartment since I was four. I love it. It's my haven." I don't tell him the second part of the story. *Oh, and I'm about to lose it. Which feels like the absolute worst thing that could happen to me in the entire world.*

Noah tilts his head, reading something in my tone. "What's the problem? You have a high-powered finance job and live in an apartment you love. But there's trouble in paradise."

I take a drink from my water glass. I need to pace myself. "No trouble." Admitting all that would be way too much for a blind first date with a guy whose last name I don't even know. "Tell me about you." What to ask? I remember Grace's scolding. *Talk about your favorite book, your favorite movie, your favorite artist. Just let the conversation flow naturally.* "Seen any good movies lately? Who's your favorite artist?"

Noah laughs. "All right, Irish. We'll keep the conversation neutral. For now." He considers my questions for a second. "Let's see, I haven't seen a movie in several years. I've been too busy with work. Favorite artist: that's hard, but Picasso is definitely up there. The genius is just so obvious. I guess I'm partial to the Impressionists. I've always liked the drama of a good Delacroix and the unashamed romance of a Renoir. How about you?" Like he's playing a game.

"Matisse. And Hockney."

He nods. "On our next date we can hit the Met. It's not far from my apartment."

"Careful," I warn him. "That's getting a little too close to an actual address."

"Oops," he grins. *Wow, he's sexy.*

I watch as his fingers weave through mine. He's holding my hand like people do in Central Park when they're relaxed on a sunny day and happily in love. *This man is downright dangerous.* "You know, you're not what I was expecting," I tell him.

"No?" Light mischief plays in his eyes. "What were you expecting?"

Oh Jesus. His blue eyes are *actually* twinkling.

This is not good.

Either that, or it's the best thing that has ever happened to me.

Stop thinking what you're thinking, L. Emerson, some logical inner voice scolds me sternly. *Stop telling yourself you might not need that spur-of-the-moment trip to Ireland after all.*

"I don't know, but not…" I wave my hand across the whole…*look* of him. "…*this.*"

More twinkling. "Are you disappointed?"

"Of course I'm not. It's just that now Grace is going to be unbearably smug."

"So's my brother. Because of…" he waves his hand over me, copying my gesture. "…*this*."

I take another sip of water and, as I do, Noah's phone buzzes on the table with an incoming text.

Cleo.

He clicks the lock button so the screen goes black. "Sorry about that." But then it lights up again with another text.

Sloane.

He clicks the lock button again.

"You're a popular guy, Mr. Steel," I joke, trying to laugh it off.

"It's just work. They're checking up on me."

I shrug a little. It's none of my business who texts Noah Steel.

Yet another text pops up.

Amanda.

Noah takes his phone and shoves it into his pocket. "I'm going to start this blind date or whatever we're calling it by promising you that I'll always be honest with you. That last text wasn't from work. It was from a girl who wants to go out on a date with me. But I don't want to go on a date with her."

"Why not?"

"She's not what I'm looking for."

"What *are* you looking for?"

The question hits something in him and his gaze is almost too much. "You wouldn't believe me if I told you."

"Good answer," I have to admit. "Better to let a random dating app select for you instead of taking your chances on a real live human."

"I had to accept a date with *Lucky Irish*, now, didn't I? My brother told me the algorithms trawl through all your internet usage. *All* of it. From day one. And then it makes the matches based on everything it learns."

"That almost sounds creepy."

Noah gently tucks a stray curl behind my ear. With his movement, his thigh is now flush against mine, ludicrously warm and hard. My heart beats in my chest with a strange kind of longing. I can't be jealous of *Cleo* or *Sloane* or *Amanda*. I hardly know him. But for some reason maybe I am. *Because he's so freaking beautiful.*

No wonder he's popular. It doesn't make sense for him to be here at all.

His eyes meet mine with a hint of something that's more than playful. Something deeper. "*You*, Lucky Irish, have my undivided attention. Okay?" Like he's trying to reassure me.

Which I don't need, of course. "If you say so, Noah Steel."

The air between us feels electric. A light throb plays between my legs. He smells like leather and uncut… comfort.

Help. I'm drowning in the cloud of alpha male pheromones Noah Steel is emitting.

The waiter arrives with our food. Setting our plates in

front of us, he remains professional, making a point of not staring at how close we're sitting to each other, or how Noah's hand is still holding mine. "I hope you're enjoying your evening so far, Mr. Steel. Ms. Irish."

"We are," Noah confirms. "When I googled your establishment before our dinner tonight, your website mentioned a penthouse suite. Is it available tonight? In fact, is it available for the entire weekend?"

What?

"Yes, Mr. Steel, it is available. Would you like me to reserve it for you?"

"Yes." Noah hands the waiter a black credit card. "Make sure everything goes on this. We'd like to have dessert on the rooftop."

"Of course, sir."

15

THE WAITER RUSHES off to organize Noah's request.

"Penthouse suite?" I nudge him gently with my elbow. Out of nerves mainly, but also because I can't think of anything else to say. "Just because I told you about my secret fantasy doesn't mean I want it to happen tonight."

Oh my god, did I just say that out loud?

Like we're old chums enjoying an inside joke?

That happens to be about me not only getting laid but also knocked up?

What the hell!

He nudges me back, soothing my panic by a single degree. "It's just dessert, Irish. Don't get overexcited."

I give him a look but I can feel that my face is pink. "I'm not...*overexcited.*" *Stop talking now!*

The soft notes of humor and a kind of familiarity that

shouldn't be there buffer his joke: "Don't worry, I'm not offering to be your sperm donor—not yet, at least."

"Very funny."

"I just thought it might be nice to have a view for our second half of the evening."

I don't know why the word *evening* sounds so filthy in his deep, husky voice. Or why *second half* sounds both daunting and electrifying. *Or why my panties are saturated.* "I guess…it would." But dessert doesn't take the whole weekend, is what I'm thinking.

Reading my thoughts, he muses, "Our options are wide open. Isn't it glorious?"

"Options?" Glorious?

"Yes. Options, Irish. It's not a dirty word."

"I know, but—"

"Relax. Eat your dinner."

I have no idea why, but the lightly bossy command makes something inside me sort of…*clench* with a weird, brimming pleasure.

How does he do that?

I've been a good girl and a dutiful one all my life. But right now I feel my mother's Irish spark lighting up.

I'm tired of always being good. I want to let my wild side run free, for once in my life. I'm Lucky Irish tonight, not L. Emerson, not Lucky Ashton. I can do whatever I want.

"We can stay right here if you prefer," he says. "It's up to you."

More of that perceptive kindness. Laced as it is with

graveled bass notes and dark promises, Noah Steel might as well be mainlining hundred-proof aphrodisiac into my veins.

Which is a first. I went to a strait-laced all-girls high school and spent all my free time studying, completing internships that were organized for me, and then training for the job I would one day take over. I have no experience with aphrodisiacs whatsoever.

"No. I want to," I hear myself reply. "I want to see the rooftop."

"Good." He nudges me playfully again, adding, "My driver can take you home whenever you want. No pressure to start fulfilling your wildest dreams at all."

"You're really making me regret confiding in you, Steel." But his banter is so genuinely kind, I don't feel any actual regret at all.

"I'm sorry," he laughs. "I'll try not to mention babies, sperm or Earth Mothers again this evening."

"Thank you." But some deep, instinctual yearning flares.

He has a driver. And he didn't even blink at the thought of booking a five-star penthouse suite for an entire weekend. I'm starting to get the feeling money is no object for Noah Steel. Not that that's unusual for a finance guy in New York City, but still. He's particularly blasé about it.

The food is beyond delicious. Between the champagne, the exceptional meal, the heat of Noah's leg pressed up against mine and the thought of heading up to the balcony of *our own private penthouse*, I'm in a haze of… well, having the best night I've had in a very long time. Or maybe ever.

He's charming, sexy as all hell, unashamedly masculine, funny, and so easy to be with I forget about my nervousness and just relax into how nice it is to spend time with him.

I learn that he works with his brothers, he travels frequently and his apartment has a nice view.

But we're careful, almost like we're playing a game. Like whoever can keep the information we're sharing as non-revealing as possible wins.

The waiter returns with a small leather folder and places it on the table. "Mr. Steel, Ms. Irish, the penthouse is ready for you whenever you'd like it. Here's your card, room key cards, the Wi-Fi password and a QR code with our room service menu, which is also available in your room. I hope you enjoy dessert."

Noah's not looking at the waiter when he says it. He's looking at me. "I know I will."

16

NOAH

I'm TRYING to keep my cool here, but there's a slow burn in the middle of my chest that feels very much like a wild new obsession is currently taking hold inside my heart. Gripping it like a fist.

Everything about her is charming me. Every sweep of her long eyelashes, every exasperated huff of laughter, every sweet glance.

I didn't expect it to be so fucking *sudden*.

So ragingly all-consuming.

So goddamn *sure* of itself.

It's insane that I'm sitting here wondering if I've just met the love of my life. Not even wondering. *Knowing.*

No one can know such a thing after a grand total of two hours.

But I do. She's the one.

After a lifetime of wondering and hoping, searching

but never finding, this feels like a lightning-bolt-shaped Cupid's arrow has pierced me directly in my hot-beating heart.

Which sounds cheesy as fuck.

My problem is…I *like* cheese. I've fucking *craved* true romance for as long as I can remember. Life has always disappointed me in that regard. Like it's been preparing me for this exact moment, so I *know*. So there's no fucking mistake about it.

You're too picky, my brothers used to tell me.

Who are you waiting for?

The perfect woman doesn't exist.

Circumstance has proven all three of my brothers wrong. And it's happening to me right now in real time.

I'm fucking falling in love.

With a total stranger.

A total stranger who happens to be as perfect as anyone I've ever come across. Like fate has thrown all the minutiae of a human being I never thought to wish for—that are specific to *me* and only me—into some bubbling cauldron, stirred them up, added several pinches of addictive, habanero-level spice and poured the whole cocktail into one living, breathing…Lucky Irish.

There's nothing to find fault with.

Nothing.

I've heard of algorithms doing their job but this is ridiculous.

Her skin is creamy-smooth, lightly tanned and glowing. I've counted the freckles dotted across the bridge of her nose. There are eleven of them. Which happens to be my lucky number.

Her eyes seem to change color depending on her mood. They get darker when I tease her. In certain plays of the light, they almost look violet.

Her hair is outrageous. Shiny and silky but thick. A golden, luminous color you might expect to see on a mythical creature. As though her Uber happened to be a white Pegasus that flew in from Mount Olympus or some magical place with rainbows and pots of gold. County Cork on steroids, maybe. I don't fucking know.

Her mouth. It's so damn luscious-looking I'm seriously in agony.

It's not only the physical draw but an emotional one that's equally intense. She's kind, that's easy to read. And smart. With a sparked, sweet but also feisty sense of humor that somehow meshes perfectly with my own.

She's a little bit lost. And it's that part of the equation that digs into me almost more than any other. I want to protect her and shield her from life's harsher edges with a ferocity I hardly recognize.

"Can I ask you a question?" I really am dying to know.

"Depends on what it is," she replies coyly.

"You don't have any other kind of relationship going on anywhere, do you?"

"Relationship?"

"Boyfriend. Broken-hearted ex. Secret husband. I don't know. I'm just trying to figure out why every man in New York isn't banging down your door."

"Of course not." All innocently. "I wouldn't have gone on a date with you if there was. There's no one."

"Why not?" I can't wrap my head around it.

"I don't know. I've been busy."

"Doing what?"

"Working. There were a lot of…expectations."

"From who?"

"My father."

I know the feeling. "I can definitely relate to that."

"Are you the oldest of your brothers?"

"Second oldest."

"So you didn't get the worst of it."

My smile is rueful. "No. I got the second worst of it. Although the third brother claims he got the worst, only because he and my father were similar people and they clashed because of it. And the fourth brother claims *he* got the worst of it because he was basically an afterthought."

She's quiet for a few seconds, waiting for me to give her more.

But that would be against the rules. "Are you and your father similar people, Lucky Irish?"

"I tried to be what he wanted. But I've always been more like my mother."

"The O'Callahan from County Cork."

Lucky smiles, but there's a sadness at the edges of it I really can't handle. "Exactly."

"I was the brother who was most like our mother. And the Sullivans from Dublin."

This earns me a real smile. "That must be why the algorithms matched us."

"Must be."

I can't wait any longer. I would generally consider myself a nice, level-headed and mostly considerate guy, but there's nothing *nice* about my craving. It's feral and voracious. My need to taste her feels madness-edged.

Slowly, I slide my hand under her hair, around the nape of her neck. She lightly gasps as I very gently squeeze and the sound makes my cock fully hard.

It's *intense* finding the girl of your dreams.

I want her happy and giggling and so blissed out she'll never want to leave me.

I want to protect her, ravage her and fucking *please* her so ferociously I feel like I've morphed into a love-struck caveman who's only mission in life is to deliver mind-blowing orgasms and romantic happily ever afters.

Staring into her starry eyes, I've found what I've been looking for. It's as simple as that.

"I'm going to kiss you now, Lucky Irish. Are you ready for me?"

"No," she whispers. But her lips part in anticipation. "I need to warn you about something."

"What?"

Her teeth gently bite into her plump bottom lip.

Fuck. "Tell me."

"I've never really done…anything like this. Like I said, I've been too busy."

"Too busy to kiss?"

She nods. "Too busy to do anything at all."

"Anything at all?" Like, *anything?*

"Anything," she confirms.

She's a fucking *virgin?*

Holy hell, I am so done for.

I lean in, brushing my lips against hers before I settle in more deeply. Her breathy coo as I dip my tongue into her mouth and get my first taste is enough: I'm fucking hooked.

She tastes like champagne and paradise.

She tastes like my wildest dreams—and I never *had* wildest dreams before right now. I never dared to. Because everything and everyone was just so disappointing.

Until Lucky Irish showed up.

And now *her* wildest dreams are *my* wildest dreams. This girl, happy and round and pink-cheeked, full of my cum and knocked up with my babies.

Fucking hell, Maddox.

A few days ago I was helping old ladies cross the street.

Now all I want to do is to *breed* this little virgin by

giving her so much pleasure she'll have no choice but to fall madly in love with me.

I fully realize I might have lost my mind. No one falls in love this fast. It's impossible. I'm sure I'm just worked up because I've gone too long without. My subconscious is hell-bent on getting what I promised it when I made my decision earlier this week and is now tricking me into *feeling* so much because my cock is so fucking hard and needs what it needs.

This is lust, that's all. Really, really extreme lust that's the result of living like a monk for too long.

But how is she so fucking *ideal?*

I'm probably just seeing what I want to see because I've already made up my mind that this is happening tonight.

If she agrees to it.

I know she will.

I lean in to whisper in her ear. "Irish?"

"Yeah?"

"I want this to happen. I'm telling you the honest truth when I say you are without a doubt the most beautiful girl I have ever seen in my life. I want to take you upstairs and we can have a drink and some dessert and get to know each other. We'll take it as slow as you want. You can change your mind at any time. Just say the word and I'll take you home. But I don't think you will change your mind. I think you're going to love what I'm about to give you. And I want nothing more right now than to give you every fucking thing you've ever wished for. I want to spend the weekend with you. I'll take good care of you."

Her blue eyes round. "You will?"

"Of course I will. I'm Noah, remember? Trustworthy. Patient but not too patient. Incredibly thorough. Maybe a little bit of a control freak but that can be a good thing in certain situations."

Her cheeks get that warm pink flare as her eyes hold mine. "It can?"

"Yes. It can."

She's saucy without even trying. Curious. She's navigating all the new feelings I'm inspiring. "What kind of situations?"

"The kind where I give you a lot of orgasms."

It's barely a whisper. "Oh."

Slowly, I lean in close to her ear, whispering in a low growl. "Are you wet for me?"

You're rushing this.

I can't *not* rush this. I'm too fucking hot for her.

Just when I think maybe I've pushed her too fast, my Irish dream girl shyly nods.

"Yeah?"

She barely nods again, almost submissively.

I lean closer to her ear as I place my palm on her bare thigh. I very lightly lick her earlobe and gently bite, which makes her squirm against me. "Do you want me to *feel* how wet you are for me?"

She exhales a soft breath, something between a laugh, wild curiosity and disbelief.

"You can say *yes, Noah*. Or you can say no. My advice —and I'm a Noah, so you should definitely take it: always say yes."

Lucky's eyes are dazzlingly blue as she meets my gaze, and my challenge. "Okay, then, *Noah*," she whispers. "*Yes.*"

"Good girl." My whispered growl in her ear is low and husky. My palm slides higher and she whimpers, the sound driving me very close to the edge of control. Fuck, this girl makes me crazy. I'm supposed to be a gentleman. *At least wait until you get upstairs, you maniac.* Instead, I hear myself murmur gruffly, "I think you want me to slide my fingers under those wet panties and play with your slippery little clit until you come hard right here at the table. What do you think?"

She softly inhales, like she can't believe I just said that.

"Give me a yes, Irish. We're slowly working up to your wildest dreams here, remember? No one can see us, but you're going to need to keep it down. No screaming. Do you think you can do that?"

"I don't know. I've never…"

"Never what?"

"You know."

"What?"

"Just forget it." Those light flags of pink on her cheeks get even pinker.

"Wait a minute. You mean…you've never had an *orgasm*?"

"No."

I'm shocked. How is such a thing possible in this day and age? "Why not?"

"I just…couldn't. I mean, I've tried, but I just… haven't. I can't." She pretends to shield her eyes. "God, kill me now. I can't believe I just told you that."

I carefully tuck a curl behind her ear. "Hey, it's me. You can tell me anything. It's good this way, you'll see. They wouldn't have been as good as the ones I'm about to give you anyway." I sound cocky, but it's true. I happen to have a gift. *Thank you, universe, for delivering me this little lucky charm, who just keeps astounding me with her checklist of things I didn't even know were ideal to me until she started showing me, one by one.* "Challenge accepted, Lucky Irish."

I gently nudge her shoulder with mine in that playful way we have. She huffs a laugh. Like she doesn't believe me.

My girl. Mine. "You're going to like this, Irish. Are you ready?"

17

HOLY SHIT.

Is my dreamy blind date really about to give me my first orgasm?

In the middle of a restaurant?

Earth to Lucky: have you lost your mind?

No. But I *have* discovered the key to my Irish wild side. His name is Noah Steel.

When the universe delivers *this* much hotness into your evening, sometimes you just have to go with it. My whole life, I've toed every single line it's possible to toe. I've *never* done something so wild and reckless that it rocks my world. This beautiful stranger feels like he's been put here just for me, to do exactly that.

Behind his eyes there's a depth and a dark, playful sense of humor I'm half in love with already. He's a once-in-a-lifetime discovery, you can just tell: that rare phenomenon where your personalities click and your pheromones mingle in a perfect, sparked harmony. The crazy sex appeal only compounds my problem. Not to mention the six-foot-something, beefed-up masculinity on steroids.

Noah's warm hand slides higher up my thigh.

He leans closer and my lips part because I can barely breathe. The anticipation becomes everything about me.

Very gently, one of his hands slides around the nape of my neck as the other slides even further up my thigh. He's big, ridiculously strong and controlling in the best kind of way. Quivering excitement pools in the slippery depths of my body. I can feel that my panties are saturated.

Help.

His scratchy jaw brushes against my cheek. Then his lips settle over mine and exert a gentle pressure, opening my mouth with his. Lust-drugged, I take him willingly. *God, he tastes good.* Like mint and champagne, like love and magic. With his other hand, his fingers glide over my panties, slowly centering. *There.*

Oh my god.

"You *are* wet, baby girl," he murmurs, amusement and lust adding to the smoky allure of his voice. "You *sure* you want this? Because I'm about to slide my fingers under these ruined panties, Irish. And once I do, there's no telling how far I'll go. I might even have to slide *inside*, to see how slippery that sweet virgin pussy is for me." He growls this *as* he continues to rub me gently with his rough fingers. Flutters of deep, insanely pleasurable warmth are teasing heat in one forward direction.

His movements slow.

No.

I need him to keep going.

I look into those sparkling, dark-lit blue eyes and I realize he's waiting for me to beg. I'm practically slumped against his big body in our cozy private booth and I don't care. I don't care about anything except what he's doing to me. "*Please.*" I *need* whatever tidal wave he's building to give me what it's promising. "*Please, Noah Steel.*"

I don't know why I say his whole name. His fake name. *This game we're playing doesn't feel like a game anymore. It never really did. It feels like the realest thing in the world.*

"That's my good girl. Always say yes. You're getting good at this."

Noah kisses me. His tongue slides deeper, tasting me unhurriedly. The kiss is sweet and hot and incredibly self-assured.

Noah Steel knows how to freaking *kiss.*

I really am embarrassingly inexperienced. I've kissed a few boys, but it was always in a perfunctory kind of way. Two at strictly-chaperoned dances in high school. Three good night kisses after awkward first dates in college I knew would never lead to a second. I was too distracted by the other demands on my time. And none of those boys appealed to me at all. I was always glad when the dates ended. I thought maybe I was just too uptight or too lonely or too fast-tracked by my career circumstances to find a match.

This kiss isn't like any of those. It's a kiss that promises everything. Not only tonight or the weekend, but all of it. It's the kind of kiss that makes you believe that lust is the perfect wave but love is the ocean.

I can't explain it. All I know is that neither one of us is hesitating. There's no fumbling or rushing, just a hunger that's wildly sure of itself and perfectly in sync.

His fingers slide *under* the lace of my panties.

It's simply the most profound thing that's ever happened to me in my life. His fingers swirl over my clit, teasing in small, slow-moving circles, pinching and squeezing with gentle, expert precision. Dipping inside me before continuing his slippery caresses.

Oh my god, it's happening.

"Fuck, you're beautiful," he murmurs. "So sweet and fucking *ready* for me, Irish."

His tongue pushes into my mouth as the curl of pleasure he's working with his fingers reaches a crazily high peak, then breaks into tight, shattering bursts of pure, mind-blowing ecstasy. He catches my moan. "That's my girl," he's murmuring. "My gorgeous little Lucky."

Noah works my pleasure unhurriedly, his mouth and his hands playing me like Yo Yo Ma plays his goddamn cello.

I'm drunk on him. I think I might be in love with him. My body adores him, spasming in long, lush ripples.

As the rapture slowly starts to calm, I let my fingers wander across the rough surface of his jaw. He kisses me with a tender need that feels almost like adoration, like he's as drugged as I am.

"Noah," I say softly.

"Yeah?" His voice is deep and rasped.

"That was..." I can't even speak. I'm still riding the intense, lingering rushes.

"...just the beginning, baby girl. It gets even better."

"It does?" I manage to gasp.

"Of course it does." Holding my gaze, Noah licks his fingers. "Let's get started on the next one of those wildest dreams."

18

———

Lucky

NOAH SMOOTHS my dress back in place. He tucks another errant curl into place. Then he takes my hand and escorts me through the restaurant. We pass the maître d' and Noah thanks him.

"The penthouse has its own private elevator, Mr. Steel. Just down at the end of that hallway."

Private elevator. Private penthouse. And a whole weekend with Noah Steel.

As soon as the elevator doors close, sealing us into our own world, Noah's thumb slides along my jaw. "Remember what I told you. I know this is happening fast, because I think I might already be obsessed with you, Lucky Irish, but you can slow me down anytime with a single word."

"Yes?" I might be teasing him. Because I'm dazed and high on my endorphin rush after that life-changing orgasm he just gave me. For the first time ever, I'm not second-guessing anything. All my hesitations have been swept away by my new discovery of *the things he can freaking do*.

The realization is shockingly sure of itself.

I want him to be the one. Tonight. Now.

I'm going to cash in my V-card with Noah Steel.

"*Yes* isn't going to slow me down, baby girl. In fact it might make me go a little crazy. Just to give you fair warning."

My body is still humming. I feel hot and reckless. "How crazy?" I whisper.

Noah leans me back against the wall of the elevator. "Very. Fucking. Crazy." His eyes glimmer with that sparked playfulness and a dark, brimming desire.

There's a power to this I wasn't expecting. He's so damn *big*, his grip ludicrously strong. He could so very easily overpower me. In any other place or time this might unsettle me. But with Noah, I can feel it lighting me up. I *want* to tempt him so much I hardly recognize myself.

I stand on my toes and lightly touch my tongue to his plump bottom lip. His mouth takes mine in another hungry, tender, desperate kiss and I gasp, my body arching into him.

Damn, that algorithm really nailed it. This chemistry is combustible.

His hands grasp my hips, pulling me against his hard

body. He slides a muscled thigh between mine. I can feel his arousal pressing hotly against my stomach.

Holy shit.

He's *huge.*

I don't have much—okay, any—experience with these things, but I'm not *that* naïve.

The feel of his massive *manhood* does strange things to me. It basically distills me down to my basest female urges. He knows my secrets. He gave me my first orgasm, a full-body bloom that reached all the way down to my soul and lit a new bonfire inside me. He owns a piece of me now. Our bond is real.

I want him like I've never wanted anything.

Noah lifts me easily and his brute strength sends a warm thrill to my still-rippling core. "Which one of those wildest dreams should we attend to next?"

It's a joke, probably, and it *needs* to be a joke. We're hardly going to start working on the wildest dreams I confessed to him *tonight.* We hardly know each other.

Even so, I wrap my arms and legs around him as he kisses me again. The gigantic ridge inside his jeans presses into my stomach and I writhe a little, without meaning to, needing more.

Jesus. He's so freaking big.

"That's my good girl." The husk of his deep voice is the sexiest thing I've ever heard. "You want to come again so fucking bad. You're trying to get off by rubbing that sweet, wet pussy against my big cock, aren't you, baby?"

Oh hell. Yes. Yes I am.

The elevator doors slide open and Noah carries me into the suite. All I can think is *thank God because I can't wait another second for more of what he can do.*

It's dark except for the glow of a few low lamps and the city outside the wall of windows. I can vaguely appreciate that the room is palatial and very luxurious.

Noah lays me onto the bed, crouching over me. My arms and legs are still wrapped around him. He holds his weight as his mouth takes mine in another brain-demolishing kiss.

As he kisses me, he lays the full weight of his big body onto mine. My dress has ridden up, my panties are saturated, my legs are wrapped around him and now he's pressing the length of that colossal hardness against me, forcing my body to cradle him *very* intimately.

Staring into my eyes, Noah grinds his big cock against my clit, still slick and hyper-sensitive from the orgasm he already gave me. The rhythmic force of him tips me over another crazy edge. The pleasure blooms in an over-flowing swell that crashes through me, each wave more intense than the last. *"Noah. Noah,"* I hear myself moan.

Okay, I'm officially hooked on this man. I really never knew pleasure could be so extreme.

"Good girl. You're so fucking *hot* for me, Irish." The smug smirk somehow entwines with his awed gaze as he stares down at me and smooths my hair, that damn twinkle in his lust-dark eyes. "You okay?"

Once I can manage it, I shake my head.

"No?" His smugness immediately turns to concern. "If you want to take a little break we could order some—"

"*No.*" I'm clinging to him as the pleasure still ripples. I *need* him. I need him to anchor me. You don't come *that* hard twice in a row without needing someone to hold onto. I'm new at this. I'm adjusting to being enlightened and reborn.

I can feel his low chuckle, *there*, where I'm still coming. "Okay, Irish, I get you. You want me to make you come again."

Slowly, I nod.

"Greedy girl. I can't blame you for wanting to fast track all those wildest dreams though. Let's level up."

Level up? *There's an up?* Then again, of course there is. We haven't even gotten to the main event yet.

I need it now. All this time I've been missing out on *this*. This big, manly *beast* who can make me come so hard with barely a wink of those blue, blue eyes. "Please," I whisper.

I don't even know what I'm begging for. I just want to *feel*. More of this. More of *him*. After a lifetime of stepping up, playing nice, being alone most of the time and doing whatever I was fucking told, I want to be *free*. I don't know how Noah Steel does it but that's exactly how he makes me feel. Free and safe and so damn good I'm already addicted.

"You're in good hands, little Irish. I'm going to take such good care of you. Now, be a good girl for me while I take off your dress. Are you ready for me?"

"Yes."

Noah takes off my dress. He unclasps my bra and pulls it off, murmuring a low oath when he sees me. "My perfect, perfect dream girl. I can't believe I found you."

19

———

NOAH

THE UNIVERSE MIGHT BE PLAYING tricks on me, for all I know. I'm half expecting to wake up. To realize that my imagination has fabricated this girl out of thin air and that she'll suddenly disappear into the hazy mist of some desperation-induced daydream.

But I know for a fact my imagination could never have created such a sublime creature as Lucky Irish.

Her breasts are full and creamy-smooth, her pink nipples taut and rosy. Her stomach is graceful and femi-nine, not overdone in an abs-of-steel or overworked-gym-bunny kind of way, but natural and womanly. It's a detail that undoes me. All that talk of babies and surrounding herself with magical little children has shifted something inside me. You hear it on the internet all the time and the phrase might as well be a flashing neon sign inside my brain. *When you know, you know.*

I want to be the one to do it.

I'll do it right fucking now if she'll let me.

I want to plant my seed right here in this perfect girl, with a ferocity I've never experienced before.

I'm slayed by the fucking *magnitude* of her gorgeousness. And by how perfect she is for *me*. I want her, it's as simple as that. Not just tonight, but all of it. *The knocked up Irish dream girl. The magical babies. A full-to-the-brim home full of laughter, something we both missed out on.* I'm never letting this girl out of my sight. I need to convince her to let me give her everything I have.

I almost wish I'd fucking taken care of myself before the date. I'm on fire. My heart pounds against my ribs, like it's grown too big to fit comfortably in there. And it's not the only thing that's uncomfortably fucking big. My cock is hot and painfully engorged.

Lucky Irish somehow makes this whole experience very new.

Finally. Sex with a woman I want to keep.

All my life, I've gone with the flow. I've allowed relationships to happen because it's what you do when you're young, in demand and you don't want to be alone. But the romantic in me always held something back, because I always knew I wasn't with the person I wanted to end up with.

I take her nipple into my mouth like it's my very first time—and it might as well be for the overload of obsession-fueled lust coursing through my veins. I suck on her slowly, worshipfully, in awe of the silky softness of her.

I usually consider myself an easy-going guy. I'm the diplomat in my family. The mediator. The one my brothers come to when they need something handled with a level head.

In the bedroom it's a slightly different story. I've been told I'm a "beast," an "animal," "the Superman of orgasms," and "the best fuck in New York"—among others. By women who were placeholders. I don't sleep around so I tend to get pent-up from time to time. And I happen to have won the lottery in the well-hung department. It is what it is.

Now, with Lucky Irish in my bed, I'm fucking feral.

She tastes like nothing I've ever experienced. Sweet. Almost floral. Like milky honey blossoms in the garden of Eden. I suck on her like I'm trying to drink this essence from her. I'm demanding. It's perverse, almost, the need and greed I feel.

Little moans of pleasure escape her, getting me even harder.

I take my time, licking, feasting, peeling off her panties with my teeth.

I ease her legs wider and position her so her legs are wrapped around my shoulders. I hold her thighs apart. "Look at you, baby girl, so wet for me. I'm going to taste you now. And eat you until you come so hard you're going to see stars as you scream my name."

"Eat...?" she breathes, like she's shocked I would suggest such a thing. Her gasp comes out sounding like, *"Oh, fuck."*

There's a smile on my face when I take my first taste of her. I'm literally in heaven. I feast greedily on her sweet softness and she moans, her hands grabbing fistfuls of my hair.

I don't hold back. I couldn't if I tried. I eat into her like a man possessed, zeroing in on her clit, licking and sucking her in soft pulls as my fingers tease and explore.

She starts to quiver. Her hips sway gently in a back-and-forth rhythm. She cries out my name.

I fucking love that sound like I've never loved anything. Of her dreamy exhale, calling to me, like I'm a mythical god she's already in love with. Like I'm too good to be true.

Her pussy pulses around my tongue and the taste of her as she comes becomes the most feverish addiction I've ever known.

She's mine. I want to marry her and give her ten babies and spend the rest of life doing *this*.

Mine, mine, mine.

20

———

Lucky

Wave after wave of mind-blowing pleasure throbs hotly through my entire being. I hear a low sound and realize it's me. I'm moaning his name.

Holy hell, he's good at this.

Noah takes his time, licking more gently now. He kisses my clit, causing another deep ripple of bliss. Then he kisses his way up my body, lying next to me with his head propped on a burly arm. His smug grin is so hot and also sort of endearing because he looks so happy, I can't stop myself. I fall a little bit in love with him.

He's still fully clothed. I'm naked, wet and quivering from coming so freaking hard—and I'm *still* coming. I feel vulnerable in a way that turns me on even more. I'm at the mercy of this big, sexy beast and my inner newly-awakened sex goddess *loves* this. I want him to *use* me so much, it feels like I was born for exactly this reason.

When I consider my wildest dreams, it kind of *is* what I was born to do.

It's interesting when you think about it. I've fought for my feminist rights my whole life. I always will. But right now the only thing I care about is getting fucked by this gorgeous hot hunk of a man. That *is* a feminist right, after all. Using our femininity to fulfill our physical, sensual and biological urges. And right now *all* my urges are on overdrive.

The backs of his fingertips trace my cheekbone. That he can *eat me* so damn hungrily one minute and be so charmingly tender the next makes me fall in love with him even more.

Stop doing that, girl. It's too fast.

Then again, that trip to Ireland might not—

I shut my subconscious off. My inner Earth Mother who now moonlights as a sex goddess is at war with L. Emerson, who's all about common sense. I'm going to let the two of them fight it out on their own. I'm too busy right now. A very sexy almost-stranger is handing out orgasms like it's going out of style.

"Now that I've tasted heaven, Lucky Irish, I'm afraid you're stuck with me. You are outrageously, dangerously beautiful. You taste like fucking heaven on Earth."

I touch his chest, opening the top button of his shirt. "A girl could get addicted to you very, very easily, Noah Steel."

"We don't have to rush. We have all weekend—"

"I don't want to wait." I unbutton the next button. And the next, running my fingers across the hard surface of his chest. "Take this off."

He pulls off his shirt.

Whoa.

He's buff *as hell.* His shoulders are wide, his chest and arms powerful and sculpted. His skin is sun-tanned and warm-looking. I'm surprised to find he has a tattoo of a diamond-patterned snake curled around one shoulder. "What the hell, Steel, you're *crazy* hot."

"You want more of me, baby?"

I nod. *Of course I do. I want everything.* "Yes."

"Good girl. Keep going."

"A snake?" My fingers rove over his ink. It's beautifully drawn.

"I'm the stealthy brother. The one you'll never see coming."

I smile at this, exploring the hair-dusted surface of his chest. "Well, *I* sure didn't see you coming." His rock-hard abs. The dark arrow line of hair that leads tantalizingly under the waistband of his jeans.

My fingers glide over the huge ridge that snakes tight-mounded under his jeans and he groans.

Fuck, he's big.

Now I get the snake.

I finger the bulging rigidity and I can feel him growing even harder. *Oh my god. How….?*

Noah reads my mind. "It will, trust me."

I'm not exactly *nervous*, I'm still riding my high and I want more of it. But I *am* in awe. "You're…a little daunting, Mr. Steel."

"You won't be daunted when you're coming hard on my big cock, sweetheart. I'll be careful with you. But not *too* careful. I'll take you higher than you've ever been. I'm a Noah, remember? I just happen to be…a very well-hung one."

I bite back a hesitant smile. But I'm so beguiled by him, my fingers continue to explore. I unfasten the top button of his jeans. "Take these off. I want to see you."

He unzips his jeans, freeing his—*holy shit!*—hot-looking *massive* cock. I mean…

"Jesus Christ," I gasp.

Noah laughs, kicking off his jeans and his boxers. He lays back, resting his head on a muscular arm, allowing me to adjust to the sight—*and the freaking size*—of him.

Noah Steel is something else. He obviously looks good in his expensive-looking clothes, but this is different. He's like a living, breathing sculpture. A very…enhanced one.

His cock is colossal, veiny and silky-looking. The rounded head leaks a bead of milky moisture and I've seriously never been so fascinated by anything in my life. My craving for him—and his enormous freaking *manhood* —is wild and ravenous. I'm *thirsty*. I want to rub myself all over him and *take him inside*.

His grin is wolfish, as though he can read this. "I'm all

yours, Lucky. You can do anything you want to me. Help yourself."

I don't feel shy. I'm too damn hot for him. He's making me feel reckless and so sexy it almost hurts.

Slowly, I wrap my fist around his huge length. With both hands, I smooth my palms along his shaft, entranced by the hard textures of him and the throbbing thickness. My fingers squeeze gently and another gush of moisture seeps.

Mine.

I swirl it.

Then I lick my finger. His eyes are as dark as blue embers. "I'm on the pill," I tell him.

"Yeah? Why?"

"What do you mean 'why'?"

"You said you're not dating anyone. And your friend set you up with me two days ago."

The question is kind of bold and very personal but, then again, so is what we're about to do. "When I started my new job I got so stressed out it messed with my cycle. My doctor said the pill might help regulate things."

"Has it?"

Also personal. So is cashing in my V-card with no barrier—and if he doesn't let me do this soon, I might start crying and begging. Anyway, it's like this with us. It's unusually easy to be completely honest and totally unfiltered. "It's starting to."

"So, a hot, sweet, sassy, gorgeous, horny as fuck little

virgin on the pill wants me to fuck her with no condom. Are you trying to kill me, Irish?"

"No." L. Emerson might almost be offended. But Lucky Irish wants *exactly* what he just described. "I just want…"

"Want what? To find out what it feels like to come so hard you scream my name and forget your own?"

Noah Steel was right about one thing. He's the easiest person to say yes to in the world. "*Yes.*" It's weirdly emotional. "I just…I want to please you and give you so much pleasure you feel like you're going crazy. Like what you do to me."

His eyes are darker than I've ever seen them, as though he's on the verge of losing control. "All right then. You asked for it. My girl gets whatever she wants. That's my job now, to make sure every single one of those wildest dreams comes true. Starting with this one. You're going to *love* this." He lays himself over me, using his strength to position me and push my legs wider.

Noah's hot, *enormous* cock slides against my slippery, still-pulsing pussy and I moan. The pleasure never really went away. It's holding on, waiting there for more of his magic to tip it over another extreme edge.

"Wrap your legs around me and hold on tight."

I obey him. He takes the head of his cock and rubs himself against my hyper-sensitive clit. He exhales a groan, like it's almost too much. "I've never had sex without a condom before, Lucky Irish. Not once. Ever. But with you, it's the only way I could."

I don't analyze what he's telling me, but I understand it. He already told me he's never loved anyone before. It's a given that I haven't either. It's probably impossible for us to already be in love. It's too fast and we hardly know each other. But the click and the chemistry and the goddamn orgasms are enough. I love being with him. I love the way he smells like leather, fresh air and smoky whiskey, as though he just stepped off a GQ photoshoot wearing wool and leather clothing and camping by a lake. Chopping wood. He smells like hot, virile *manliness* and it's more than intoxicating, it's fucking drugging. My new addiction has a mind of its own.

I love the way he tastes and the way his grip is close to painful. I love his deep, husky voice and the words he's murmuring. "You're so fucking beautiful, Lucky. You ready for me? You want me to fuck you real good?"

It's a pure, primal, maddening need. *"Yes. Yes. Please, Noah."*

Noah pushes his big cock against my soft, slick pussy, opening me. I'm tight but so wet the broad head of his cock slides inside me, stretching me. *God, he's so freaking big.*

He pushes deeper, and the stretching, slippery friction rubs a sweet, deeply pleasurable pain that makes me moan. It fucking *hurts*, but it also feels impossibly, unfathomably good.

"*Noah*," I gasp.

"You're such a good girl for me, baby. You want more? Then beg me for it."

"More. More. Please."

"I know you fucking *love* it, baby girl. Look at you, so damn pretty, taking it like a good girl. Are you going to come for me if I give you more?"

Noah's hands grip my ass, forcing me to take more of him. He's so strong I think he might leave bruises and I *want* him to. I want him to mark me as *his*.

He pushes deeper. One hand grips me. With the other, his fingers use my own trickling moisture to circle the cove of my ass. Not entering, but pressing, playing the rhythm of his drives as his huge cock thrusts deeper. And deeper. The fullness and the angle rub my clit and another sweet-hot trigger deep inside me in a synced overload of what could only be described as bliss.

The wave throbs and overflows, shattering me with star-flicked bursts of nearly-unendurable pleasure. I cry out as my inner muscles squeeze tightly around him, over and over. He thrusts into each spasm, spinning the ecstasy higher.

I can feel every ridged inch of him inside me as he fucks me so slowly and deeply I feel like he's a part of me now. We're connected and bonded forever. He's the only thing I can feel.

"Wrap your legs more tightly around me, baby girl." He's crooning to me, and I need it. I'm literally being split wide open and his soothing voice anchors me. "Pull your knees higher. That's it. You're so good at this. Look at you, taking all of my big cock like a good girl. You feel so fucking good. Come again for me, baby. I'm going to pump you full of my hot cum this time. Are you ready? How bad do you want it?"

"*Bad*," I hear myself beg.

"I know you do, you sweet, dirty girl. Come for me now. Milk my big cock with that tight, perfect pussy, Irish. Show me how hard you can come."

With my knees fully bent and wrapped around him, his thick cock pushes even deeper. He growls with a satisfied hum and I can feel that he's fully inside me now. It's uncomfortable but also life-changing. I'm a vessel to be filled by him. I've never been this happy. I've never felt this good.

His fingers dip into my ass as he works the rhythm until all the sources of pleasure converge into one cresting, crazy-ass tidal wave.

I come *hard*.

My inner muscles work his big cock voluptuously until he growls like a bear. Hot jets of his cum coax another—even higher—wave and I come even *harder*—*again,* like the orgasms are building on each other, spiraling me into an orbit of pleasure that completely undoes me.

The waves are long and lush, tugging him over and over as he pumps his hot seed deep inside me.

I'm crying his name, holding on for dear life as the earth-shattering spasms burst and ripple.

It lasts a long time.

We're locked into our grinding, sweaty frenzy, fucking and kissing like our lives depend on it. My fingernails dig into his back as I suck on his tongue. We're both breathing hard as our slick, secret bond pulses and spills. I can feel gushes of moisture where I'm overflowing with his cum.

After a while, the ripples begin to calm.

I'll never be the same, it's as simple as that.

"Noah Steel, you're a beast," I whisper. I laugh a little and I can feel the barely-there movement *inside me* where he's still so deeply wedged.

"And you're the most beautiful girl in the world, Lucky Irish. Fucking hell."

21

———

I WAKE but I don't open my eyes. I'm too comfortable. And *very* aware of a deeply pleasurable…bulk. Barely inside me.

Noah Steel.

He's spooning me. I'm wrapped in his bearhug with his huge cock wedged between my legs. I'm so warm and I feel so safe I don't ever want to move.

Except to arch slowly back, letting more of him ease inside.

And a little more.

Fuck, this man feels good.

I don't allow myself to let any of the little voices of common sense seep in. *You lost your virginity last night to a total stranger! You got tipsy off several glasses of champagne, jumped into bed within hours of meeting him and proceeded to get down and dirty like nobody's business!*

And had *a lot* of orgasms.

156

Ten. Maybe twelve. I lost count.

I need another one.

Whatever is happening to me is more powerful than reason.

I arch again, feeling the huge thickness of him getting even thicker, sliding deeper.

"Mornin', gorgeous," comes the growly murmur in my ear. "You want more of my big cock, don't you, baby girl. You're insatiable, you hot little minx. You're unbelievably beautiful, sweet little Lucky. That's my good girl, let me in. Let me fuck that tight little pussy until you come again. You love it when you squeeze around me as you moan my name."

His fingers find my clit and my nipples as he fucks me slow and deep. My body's adjusting to him. There's pain, but it warms into the kind of deep, brimming pleasure that'll drive you mad if you don't get more of it. The sheer size of him forces me to submit and surrender to being completely, totally possessed by him.

Already, it's starting.

"*Noah,*" I moan. "*Noah, I'm going to come.*"

"For me and only me, Lucky Irish. Say it."

God, I'm so close.

"Tell me how much you fucking love riding my cock, baby girl. Tell me how much you want it."

"*Fuck me hard, Noah Steel. Please make me come. I need it so much.*" L. Emerson wouldn't dream of talking dirty. But Lucky Irish fucking *loves* it. "*I love how your giant cock feels when you spill your seed inside me. I only come for you and—"*

His cock drives deep, filling me so thickly, I cry out. I writhe back against him, loving how *full he* makes me feel. My body was made for him. Every ridge and vein is somehow in tune with all the secret triggers I own. He thrusts again, forcing the pain-flicked pleasure to another insane peak as his fingers pull and swirl.

The hot wave rolls through my body. I writhe into it, riding the heat. Bucking. Crying his name. Coming so hard I wonder if I'll survive it. My pussy works him strongly until I feel the throb of him and the flooding, jetting warmth that surges and overflows.

Our crazy mating—which feels like the only word for it, it's so needy and lusty—gets more desperate each time. Like our addiction is taking a turn, digging deeper.

After a while, he lazily thrusts into the snug wetness and spins my orgasm into *another* deep, brimming rush.

Damn, the man has a gift.

I doze dreamily as he kisses, bites and licks my neck.

Once he's hard again, he rolls me onto my knees, my head resting on the pillow, knees apart, and he coaxes me into another shattering climax.

We spend the day in bed. We order room service. We talk about everything that comes into our heads. We laugh at each other's jokes. We take a shower and have more hot sex. We sit out on the roof garden for a while, and he wraps me up in the duvet and holds me on his lap, feeding me chocolate, strawberries and more champagne. Our stories and our laughter come so easily it feels like we're long-ago best friends who haven't seen each other for a while and we have a lot to catch up on.

And then we go back to bed, where Noah proceeds to take me to heights of pleasure I never knew existed. Pleasure that goes beyond physical into something close to a deep emotional catharsis.

If I'm addicted to what he can do, Noah seems sort of crazed. He's absolutely voracious. Dirty and lusty and obsessed in a way that comes wrapped in tender adoration. At one point he ties my wrists to the bed. Later, he eases me into a position where he can spank me as he's fucking me. Then does this thing to me that might actually be illegal in several states. He praises me when I come. He takes care of me after our lovemaking, washing me, murmuring sweet-dirty words and holding me as I cry in his arms because he feels so good.

I don't overthink it.

I don't care that we met yesterday.

I refuse to think beyond tomorrow.

I just let it happen.

And with every hot glance, every smile that he gets out of me so very easily, every kiss and every crashing wave of soul-touching pleasure, I fall just a little bit deeper in love with Noah Steel.

22

"Okay, so you don't go to the movies because you're too busy. You have three brothers. You occasionally go to museums and you like the Impressionists. And you're extremely good in bed. What else should I know about you? What's your favorite color?"

"Blue."

It's Sunday, maybe early afternoon. I'm in the gigantic space-age jacuzzi tub and Noah is gently, carefully rinsing my hair. He ordered us breakfast in bed, we made love again and then he ran us a bath, carrying me in and insisting on pampering me.

"What shade of blue?" I'm reclined on a molded seat in the tub with jets massaging me. My head rests on a built-in pillow. "It's my favorite color too."

"It is?" Noah's strong fingers massage my head as he rinses more shampoo from my hair.

"Yes. My living room is Mediterranean Skies and my bedroom is European Summer."

"That's very specific."

"It's one of my hobbies, poring over paint samples and wallpaper swatches. I'm a little obsessed."

"So you're going to open a high-end interior design business for very select clients when you start having all your magical babies but still want to use your creativity and occasionally re-enter the real world outside the haven of your beautiful home. But only when you feel like it."

It catches me off guard. I didn't actually go into *that* much detail about that one particular wildest dream. And he just described it in the most perfect way imaginable.

I shrug a little, feeling emotional about this even though I'm not sure why. *Because he knows you better than anyone ever has, already. And because you're completely, totally falling for him. Actually, you've already fallen.* "Maybe."

Noah smiles. "I like Lucky Irish blue. It's a blue that changes colors. When I tease you, your eyes turn violet, but when you're moaning my name they're more of a royal blue."

I splash him a little. "What color are they when I splash you?"

"Sapphire blue," he grins. "Which reminds me."

"Get in with me."

"I will. I need to find something. I bought you a present."

"When? We've been in bed all weekend."

"I got it on my way to the restaurant." He goes out into the bedroom and comes back holding a small rectangular light blue box.

"You bought me a present before you even met me?"

"Just in case I liked you."

"So…you've decided you do?"

"Mm…" He pretends to think about it. Then he leans over me and kisses me. The kiss is erotic in its familiarity. We've spent the entire weekend kissing, exploring each other's bodies and kissing some more. "I'm besotted, addicted and obsessed, so I guess that's a yes."

Noah hands me the box. "This is for you, gorgeous."

I sit up. "I don't want to get it wet."

He opens the box and pulls out a piece of what looks like costume jewelry. A blue glass tennis bracelet with large stones embedded in white gold. "It can handle getting wet. My mother used to wear one of these and she never took it off. Not even at the beach."

I'm a little shocked when he tells me that. It's kind of a big deal that he would buy me something he associates with her. "It's so beautiful, Noah. It's my exact favorite color."

"Lucky guess." He opens the clasp and holds it out. "Here. Let me put it on you."

It's definitely the glintiest piece of costume jewelry I've ever seen. He puts it on and the chunky weight of it almost makes me wonder…but no. This many real sapphires would cost...*a lot.* "Thank you, Noah Steel. I love it."

"My pleasure, Lucky Irish."

I get up from my raised underwater couch. "Sit here. Let me wash you."

Noah drops his towel.

Wow.

It's a sight I'm not sure I'll ever get used to. He really is...well built. He's perfectly proportioned. Naturally fit with the body of an athlete. An edgy one, with his ink that surprised me at first but it suits him. He doesn't have the physique of a runner or a quarterback. More like an athlete with serious stamina that might do the tackling or stop someone less solid in their tracks. He's tall and big. Toned-looking with defined abs and that manly V that frames his lean hips.

And then there's that gigantic cock that's my new favorite thing in the world.

He lays back. I slowly rub the soap over his stomach and chest.

"I booked the room for us again tonight."

"Yeah?" I've been too blissed out and distracted to worry about any of the stuff I'd usually worry about. Like check-out time. Which, now that I think about it, was probably hours ago.

"You don't have other plans tonight?" he asks.

"No."

"You'll stay with me then?"

I don't know how this happened so fast. And I've been living way too much in the moment—some of the best of my life—to worry about what happens next. I haven't let my mind go there. "Okay."

"Good. There's something else I wanted to talk to you about too."

I take his enormous, thick bulk in my hands and start soaping it, watching it harden as I do this. "It's so amazing how this happens."

Noah lets his head fall back, groaning and exhaling a laugh at the same time. "I guess it is. And I'm glad it does."

His body is so fascinating to me. He's such an outrageously masculine creature. I slide my fist along his length, captivated by everything about him. "I just never knew men were so…"

He pants as my slippery grip works him. His slow smile is back-lit by dark lust. "Men were so what?"

"*Big.*"

Another rumble of laughter escapes him. "Not all of us are this big. I got offered work as a porn star once. A girl I dated years ago knew someone in the industry."

"What?" I can't help giggling. "You mean all this time you could have been making risqué movies instead of boring old investments? At least you have a back-up option if the stock market crashes."

His low laughter is my new favorite sound. *And that husky growl when he comes.* "I think I'd rather lavish my gifts all over my little Irish blind date than share myself."

"Lucky me." I rinse him, seeing then the pearl of moisture seeping from his fully hard cock. We've been in bed together for two solid days, almost constantly connected, but there's one thing I still haven't done. "There's something I want to try."

"What thing?"

"It's only fair."

"What's only fair." It's a growl, not a question.

"I want to taste you." I play coy. "Can I?"

"Well…that depends."

I bite back my smile. "On what?"

"On how dirty you're willing to get."

"I guess, Mr. Steel…" I touch my tongue to the broad tip. He tastes milky and salty. It's hard to describe how greedy the taste of him makes me feel. He's *so* beautiful. I want to please him and drive him crazy with lust. "…that I'm prepared to get very, *very* dirty."

"*Fuck*," he groans. "*Lucky.*"

I take the head between my lips, sucking gently, licking him with my roving, flicking tongue.

"*Oh, fuck.*"

I've never had cravings like this before. My need for Noah is carnal and out of control. He's changed me. Strangely, I feel more like myself than I ever have.

My fingers explore as I suck on him, swirling the moisture with my tongue. I squeeze him gently with my fists as I glide my palms along his length, cupping him and teasing him. I can't take all of him because he's so freaking big, but I use my mouth and my hands to give him as much pleasure as possible.

I want to make him feel so good he'll never recover. I know I can. When it comes to pleasuring Noah Steel, I feel like I'm a natural.

I love the feminine power of this. He's completely at my mercy. He's *mine*. No one can make him feel as good as I can. Some innate sixth sense tells me this. Just like he has a power over me, to devastate me with his gigantic love wand as he relentlessly shows me how good he is at using it.

I knew from the beginning that we clicked, but deep down I know there's a lot more to this than that. Noah and I don't just click, we *match*. Everything about this feels like we're made for each other.

I stopped worrying about it when he gave me my first orgasm, dedicating myself to living fully in the moment. Now, all I think about is reading his pleasure. Gauging every groan and every heartbeat. I know what he likes and I use this. I suck on him like I've never been thirstier, and the truth is, I haven't. He makes me crazy.

Noah's low oath is one of surrender.

His cock starts jerking in my hands. The pumping gushes flood my mouth. Wave after wave of it. I swallow as much as I can but there's too much. It spills, wetting my face and my breasts.

The ripples calm and I drink the last surges of his release, taking my time, licking him tenderly. I can feel his seedy life force inside me. I'm full of it. It's all over me. I've been anointed with his beastly beauty and his adoring perfection. I feel sticky and blessed. I kiss his wet, still-pulsing length. It's softer now but not completely. I love the weighted bulk of it in my hands.

"Irish," he rasps. "Come here, baby."

I climb onto him and he takes me in his arms, staring at me like I'm a mythical being he can't believe. He smooths my hair. He takes my face in his warm hands and kisses my lips.

"Come home with me. Move in with me. I need you with me, Lucky Irish. Stay with me."

23

I OPEN MY EYES.

Pre-dawn light seeps through the glass door that leads out to the balcony, now closed.

God.

It's Monday morning.

My weekend with Noah Steel is now over.

But what a weekend it was.

The best of my life, if I'm being honest.

Very thoroughly cashing in V-card. Check.

Getting pampered and adored to within an inch of my life. Check.

Experiencing lust on steroids with the beastliest, dreamiest man in the world for an entire weekend. Check.

But now it's back to reality.

I need to go into the office this morning before my meeting with that asshole Cash Maddox.

It's a meeting I have to show up for. Because the asshole might either be the answer to all my prayers or the final nail in my coffin of homelessness and bankruptcy.

It'll be one or the other.

I don't want to think about any of it. I want to stay right here with Noah's burly arms wrapped securely around me. Keeping me safe from everything outside our haven.

But I can't skip my meeting, as much as I might wish my problems, my mountain of debt and Cash Fucking Maddox would go away.

I turn to look at Noah.

He's still fast asleep.

I watch him for a while, taking in all the details of him that I now know so well.

His face is peaceful in sleep and stunningly handsome. His dark hair is a glorious mess. *Like coarse silk in my hands as I grab fistfuls of it.*

His broad shoulders and muscular arms are so sculpted and strong. *So good at holding me down as he fucks me.*

His cinnamon skin. *That I've literally rubbed myself all over like a horny cat.*

The two-day-old stubble that darkens his square jaw. *That feels so scratchily good on my thighs when he eats me.*

He's so, so beautiful. So masculine and ideal.

Quite possibly the man of my dreams.

But dreams aren't going to get me out of the very real mess I'm in.

I'd love nothing more than to kiss his perfect mouth. To lick my way down his snake tattoo, all the way down to his abs and that deliciously defined V. To take his giant manhood in my mouth. To wake him up by flicking my tongue so lovingly I know he'd groan.

But if I do that we'll end up in bed for hours because we never seem to be able to get enough of each other. And then I'll be late.

I really do need to focus. A lot is riding on the meeting this morning and I need to be mentally prepared for it.

I carefully unloop Noah's arm from around my waist. He stirs but doesn't wake.

I find my dress and my bag. I texted Grace to tell her not to worry about me at some point on Friday night, but there are around a million missed calls and messages from her. Which I'll have to deal with when I get home.

The romantic bubble of our weekend feels like it's been jarringly popped. All the pressing details of my life, that I conveniently blocked out for almost three days, are now insistingly taking up all the space in my brain.

There's a small notepad and a pen on a desk.

What to say?

I wish I could live happily ever after with you right here in this room. You're the most beautiful thing that's ever happened to me and

I think I might have completely and absolutely fallen head over heels in love with you.

Right this minute, I can't think about what comes next for us.

I'm too preoccupied by what comes next for me. For my almost-bankrupt company and my about-to-slip-through-my-fingers home.

Noah Steel,
Thank you for the best weekend of my life. I have to go into work early today and I didn't want to wake you. My number is 212-555-4004. Maybe we can do it again sometime.
xx Lucky Irish

Did I mean that last line as a joke? The whole message almost sounds harsh, scrawled on this note like an afterthought. I consider adding a P.S.

I love you?

I wish I could ride your perfect, ginormous cock into the sunset?

I'm pretty sure you're my soulmate and I'm very sure nothing will ever, ever compare to you?

I almost write, *Like maybe tonight.*

But another message vibrates my phone in my bag, and it distracts me.

Before I can ride off into *any* sunsets, I really need to deal with the very real possibility that I'm about to lose everything I have. That has to be my priority right now.

I take one look back at him. I blow him a kiss.

Later, Noah Steel.

And I let myself out.

24

As my Uber weaves its way through Monday morning traffic, my brain can't help replaying every vivid detail of my weekend with Noah. Not just the X-rated moments, as hot as they were, but all the small, tender ones too.

The way he would brush a strand of hair from my face when it fell across my eyes, almost absent-mindedly. So carefully.

The way he crooned to me *as* he was blowing my mind, to calm me as he eased my pleasure higher. And higher.

All those quiet, heartfelt gestures that were so…Noah. The ones he didn't have to do but couldn't *help* doing. Because he's not only the most manly man I've ever met, but also the most empathetic. *The most built.* The most genuine. The most *real*. It all feels like such a rare combination.

I miss you already, Noah Steel.

I miss the haven of you. The all-encompassing cocoon of safety and comfort you so effortlessly provided.

I miss the hot surge of your thick, bursting cock as you held me down and gripped me, forceful and rough in the best kind of way, breaking me wide open with the kind of pleasure I never knew existed.

As I walk into my apartment building and take the elevator up, it's strange how familiar everything is, yet also so entirely different.

Because *I'm* different.

On Friday, all I could feel was the full weight of my role as the captain of my father's sinking ship, spending most of my time feeling just a little bit too alone and a lot too overwhelmed by the mountain of responsibilities and expectations I've been left to deal with mostly on my own. Most days, it's really, really heavy. Some days it's downright terrifying.

For more than two days, I haven't thought about any of those things. Not even once.

For two whole days, I felt fully *alive*. I felt cherished. Wildly *sexy*. I felt appreciated, adored and more beautiful than I've ever felt. I had *fun*. I laughed. I lived completely in the moment, like a fully-realized, technicolored version of myself, as though, before, I'd been living out my days in black and white. Noah Steel realigned pieces of myself I didn't even realize were off-kilter.

Who knew hot sex with a sincere, gorgeous beefcake could be so life-changing?

My time with Noah reminded me that I'm a real person with my own hopes and dreams that have nothing to do with the approval of ghosts. Maybe I *can* be more than just a caretaker of someone else's legacy. Maybe I should try harder to follow my own path.

I don't want to live L. Emerson's life anymore. I want to live Lucky Irish's.

Of course I can't.

My weekend with Noah was a random, dreamy getaway. Inside it, I could fantasize about realizing my own dreams on my own terms.

But now, back in the harsher light of Real Life, all my demons, who had the weekend off, are back. They cluster around me like looming shadows that take on the shapes of all my worst fears.

You won't even be able to afford to put your stuff in storage. All of it will get repo'ed or will have to be sold. Every last memento of your mother.

You'll probably have to move out of New York to somewhere cheaper. Everything will feel so foreign and empty. You won't know anyone.

A financial hole that big is going to be very hard—nearly impossible—to climb out of. Your life is about to get very, very difficult.

I hope I can see Noah again. Of course I do. I think I'm in love with him.

Even though he's basically a stranger whose real name you don't actually know.

Would he even want to see you again? Is he that hot and sweet and the perfect sex-on-a-stick cinnamon roll for all his girls? For Cleo? For Sloane? For Amanda?

I believed him when he said they're work colleagues or a girl he didn't want to date.

But what if they aren't? You don't know the first thing about who he is outside of that bedroom. A man doesn't look like Noah Steel without getting the attention of a lot of women.

I gave myself to him in a way that was new. Not just physically—and *wow*, did I give, and take—but all the way down to my heart and soul. No one has told me they loved me since two hours before the car crash that killed my mother when I was four years old. My father was too preoccupied for emotions. Besides my very busy roomie I hardly see, I've been very alone for a very long time.

Noah made me feel like I wasn't alone. It felt indescribably good. It was as addictive as the rest of him.

Can you handle losing your job, your money or lack thereof, your home and having your heart broken at the same time?

Probably not. Then again, at least you'll have a place to stay. The mental hospital.

My eyes pool with tears.

Which is crazy.

I never cry.

Shit.

I need to get a grip and focus on the hellish day I'm

staring down the barrel of. My meeting with Cash Maddox starts in less than two hours.

I'm just unlocking my front door when my phone vibrates in my bag. Again.

Taking it out—it's on 2% because I didn't charge or even look at my phone all weekend—it's a number I don't recognize.

Is it him?

What would I even say to him? *I love you, Noah Steel. But that would require allowing myself to live my own life. And right now I'm too deep in the quicksand of someone else's to be able to do that.*

I let the call go to voicemail.

As soon Grace hears the door open, she comes barreling out of her bedroom. "Lucky? Where were you? Why haven't you answered your phone all weekend?"

"Hi, Gracie."

"Have you been with Noah Steel this whole time?"

"Um...yes?"

"Holy shit, tell me everything."

"That's going to have to wait. I have a meeting at ten that I would honestly rather die than go to, but I'm doing my best to cowgirl up. I need to get ready. I was supposed to go into the office first but the traffic was terrible. I didn't know if I'd have time. I can't be late."

She walks up to me and stands in front of me, studying me intently. She takes a wild curl of my hair between two fingers. "Lucky, you're *glowing*. You're also crying. What happened?"

"He's perfect and I spent all weekend having hot sex with him."

"*What?*"

"Yeah."

"Oh my god, Luck, I can't *believe* it. I mean, I *can* because you've been gone for three days, but you finally cashed it in, this is amazing!"

"Yes. Yes, I did and yes, it was."

"Oh, honey, are you okay? Was it okay for you? What was he like?"

"He's just…I don't even know how to describe him. He's beautiful. And nice, but also, like, seriously hot. And easy to talk to. Funny. And definitely…"

"Definitely what?"

"Like…" Oh, what the hell. I need to let some of this endorphin overload or whatever it is *out*. "…*huge*. Like, *gigantic*. And really, *really* good at…everything."

"Eeeee!" Laughter bubbles out of her and she squeezes my hands excitably. "I'm so happy for you, honey. How did you leave it?"

"I…well, I left a note."

"A note?"

"He was still asleep."

"You walked *out* on him?"

"No. I just…I didn't want to wake him up."

"Has he called you since you left?"

"I'm not sure. Someone just did. But—"

"It's him! That means he's obsessed already!"

"I don't know." Actually, yes I do. *You're so fucking perfect. I'm addicted to this sweet pink pussy, baby girl…*

"Does he look like his photo?"

"He looks way, way better."

"*Oh my god.*" More squealing. "I told you, those algorithms don't lie."

"You were right."

"Did you tell him your real name?"

"No. We didn't really get to that. I think we were just…enjoying being someone else for the weekend. Just living in the moment and not giving a thought to anything else."

"Did you make a plan to meet up with him again? Tonight?"

"Not yet."

"But you'll have his number. On your call record. I bet you anything that was him. Let me see your phone."

"My phone just died. I need to charge it. And I have a lot to do today. Noah Steel is going to have to wait."

Grace is still holding my hands. "Lucky." Sort of sternly but also with the kind of empathy that makes my eyes leak even more.

"Yeah?"

"Why are you avoiding him already?"

"I'm not." I let go of her hands to wipe my tears. "It

all just happened really fast. Everything was so…*perfect.* No one's *that* ideal. There has to be a catch."

Very gently, Grace says, "Maybe there isn't. Maybe he's just a really good match for you."

"Maybe. I mean, he is. I know he is. But I have a lot on my plate right now, Grace. There are only so many risks I can handle in one day."

"That's fair. But don't be scared just because he feels like the real deal. I mean, *does* he?"

I wipe another tear. "Does he what?"

"Does he feel like the real deal? Or just a really good fuck buddy?"

It's no use. The tears just keep on falling. "He feels like both. Gracie, I could fall in love with him. So easily. I feel like maybe I already have and it's giving me vertigo. Who does that after one weekend after just meeting some-one? I barely even know the guy."

Grace hugs me. It helps. I'm sobbing like a baby. I haven't cried like this…since I *was* a baby.

"It's okay to be freaked out, Luck. It's a lot. I get it. Ethan just asked me to move in with him."

"He *did?*"

She nods. "After two dates."

"Well, at least you won't be homeless if I have to hand this place over to the evil brothers who are about to toss me a lead-weighted life raft."

She holds my shoulders, squeezing lightly. "Whatever

happens, I'll be here for you in any and every way you need me to be."

"Thank you, bestie. You're the best friend in the world."

"No, you are. Now go and charge your phone, take a long, hot shower, go to your meeting and we'll figure out the rest of it tonight. Including what to do about Noah Steel."

I nod, wiping more tears. She notices then the bracelet dangling from my wrist. She takes my arm. "What is this?"

"He gave it to me. It's just—"

"Is this real?"

"No. Of course not."

Grace looks at the bracelet more closely. "Lucky. Did I ever tell you I worked in a jewelry store for a few months during that summer before I started my MBA?"

"I think…you might have mentioned it."

"They made us study gemstones. It was part of our training. These are real sapphires, Lucky. This is *real*."

I pull my arm gentle from her hold. "They can't be."

She grabs my arm again, taking the bracelet between two fingers to get a better look. "What color was the box?"

I think about it for a second. "Blue."

"Like…*duck egg* blue?"

I know my blues. "Yes. Exactly."

"Lucky." Staring into my eyes. "This is a *sapphire tennis bracelet* from *Tiffany's*. A fucking *real* one."

"Are you sure? But—"

"Holy shit, Luck. A man who looks like that *and* he's fun *and* he has a gigantic cock *and* he bought you a Tiffany bracelet? Maybe it's worth taking a little bit—or a lot—of a risk, sweetie. You *have* to call this guy back."

I'm staring at the bracelet, shocked. *Why?* He said he bought it before he even met me. "You know what my father used to tell me to be careful of when it came to analyzing business deals?"

"What?"

"He said that when something seems too good to be true, it always is."

"This isn't a business deal, Lucky. It's love. And sometimes when it seems like a perfect match, it actually is."

25

NOAH

I REACH FOR HER. Before I even open my eyes, I can feel the cool emptiness on her side of the bed.

"Lucky?"

I get up. The door of the bathroom is open. She's not in there.

Or out on the balcony.

Her bag and her clothes are gone.

She fucking *left?*

Why?

Damn it, Irish. You can't just fucking leave me.

I spot a scrawled note on the desk.

> Noah Steel,
> Thank you for the best weekend of my life. I
> have to go into work early today and I didn't want

*to wake you. My number is 212-555-4004. Maybe
we can do it again sometime.*
 xx Lucky Irish

Maybe we can do it again sometime?

What the fuck?

I find my phone. There are dozens of missed calls and messages but I ignore all of them. I key in Lucky's number, then punch the call button.

Please answer it, baby girl.

It rings eight times then goes straight to voicemail.

Hi, it's Lucky. Please leave a message. Her angel's voice makes my heart hurt.

"Lucky, I'm going to forgive you for walking out on me because it's Monday and you said you have a busy day. However, I need to see you again tonight, so don't even think about not answering my calls. Answer me, Irish. Or, even better, call me back. That's an order. It was the best weekend of my life too, baby girl. That means something. You're so fucking beautiful. Please. Call me back. I need to see you."

Fuck.

I get dressed in a rush, take the elevator down to the front desk and check out. I can't get a cab right away so I walk the few blocks back to my apartment, practically running, like a fucking lunatic, holding my phone in case she calls.

A text comes through and I feel almost dizzy with relief.

But the text is from Cash.

> Don't forget about the meeting with
> Ashton Holdings at 10. Where are you?

I'm usually at the office by seven thirty. The time now is 8:49.

My phone dies.

Fuck.

I get back to my apartment. For the first time since I bought it, my first reaction to arriving home isn't calmness. This apartment has always made me feel like I've achieved everything I wanted to achieve. The multi-million dollar floor plan, the natural light, the hum of luxury, the no-expense-spared minimalist decorating, the treetops of Central Park and the city skyline have always reminded me that all our hard work has been worth it. We've achieved a level of success few people ever reach and this apartment provides me with a constant display of that.

But not today.

Today it just feels empty.

Without the sparked light Lucky Irish's presence infuses into everything, the place looks dull and stark.

I want her here.

I want to take care of her and give her everything she's ever wanted and love her so hard she can't live without me.

I want to make her laugh, lavish her with comfort and safety and make love to her until she's crying my name because I feel so fucking good. Like I did all weekend.

It wasn't enough.

It'll never be enough.

I plug in my phone and try to bring up her number but it's just the battery icon and won't let me in.

So I storm into the shower and turn it to the coldest it'll go, stripping off and stepping under the jets.

It's painful but it's what I need. I need pain. All I can feel is pain.

After an entire weekend with the most luscious, gorgeous, sexiest girl in the world—*who felt so fucking good when her slippery, ludicrously sweet body gripped my cock so tightly I had no choice but to spill inside her, again and again*—to suddenly be without her is nothing less than agony.

There was a crazy, existential triumph to spilling my seed inside her. She was the most profound kind of pleasure I've ever known. I wouldn't have put a barrier between us if someone had held a gun to my head. I needed to feel her and get as close to her as possible like I needed air. I fucking *wanted* to knock her up with a desperate, needy kind of lust I've never experienced before.

Mine. My girl. The girl of my dreams.

What if I can't find her?

Is she okay?

Where the fuck is she?

I can trace the phone, if she won't answer my calls. One of our tech guys should be able to do that for me.

Are you running from me, Irish? Why?

A thousand women stalk me. The only one I want runs.

I already feel like I'll go mad if I can't feel her again. Or hear her musical, infectious, adorable laughter. Or hold her close and tell her how beautiful she is.

Fuck, I'm really losing it.

I slam off the shower, towel myself off and find a suit in my huge walk-in closet. I don't care if I'm on time for our meeting with fucking Ashton Holdings. I don't know what they think they'll achieve by meeting with us anyway. We've made our offer, they can take it or leave it. They're dreaming if they think we'll go a penny higher than fifteen million.

Going through the motions, I put on an Armani suit and a blue tie, the closest color I can find to her eyes. But no other blue is as deep and bright and light-filled as Lucky Irish's eyes. Reality without her feels weirdly and severely unbearable.

I smooth my hair into place and check my phone, which is charged to 8%. First I text my driver and tell him to meet me downstairs. I can't hear my phone when I'm on the Ducati. In the back of a limo, I won't miss her.

I call her.

Eight endless rings. *Hi, it's Lucky. Please leave a message.* "Lucky Irish." *I'll hunt you down like a Neanderthal, sling you over my shoulder and carry you back to my cave if I have to.* "I miss your voice. I miss your lips. I miss that sweet, wet pussy like you wouldn't believe, baby girl. I miss your blue eyes and your eleven freckles. I miss those little moans you make when you're coming so hard for me. I miss your eyelashes, blinking at me. I miss everything about you. I want to take you out to dinner tonight. Anywhere you want. Somewhere neutral, if you insist. But I want to get real with you, Lucky. I wanted to talk to you about that before the weekend ended but you left before I could. I'll tell you anything you want to know. Please. Call me back. Tell me where to pick you up and I'll be there. Call me, Irish."

I hang up, staring at the phone for a few seconds like I'm willing it to ring.

Nothing.

26

NOAH

I go directly to the boardroom on the eighteenth floor. It's where we're scheduled to meet with the CEO of Ashton Holdings.

On the way, I closed the divider between the driver and myself and left three more messages for Lucky.

The little minx still won't answer me.

Which pisses me off.

I'm completely, desperately, head over heels in love with her. She's the one I want and I won't take no for a fucking answer.

How did this happen?

It's like I stepped onto a roller coaster on Friday night and completely lost control. I'm on a ride I can't get off of. I'm so besotted I feel like a completely different person, one who cares about nothing except finding her, keeping her and loving her with every fucking thing I have.

Where the fuck is she? And why won't she answer me?

Colton and Cash are waiting for me.

I walk in and they both stop what they're doing to stare at me alertly.

Both of them smirk and Colton launches straight into it. "Wow."

"Wow what." I'm in a terrible mood. I put my briefcase on the table and open it.

"Since no one's heard from you since Friday night and since you look like…"

"Like what?" I grumble.

"Like your dry spell has finally been thoroughly quenched—"

"How the fuck would you know either way." It's more of a dismissive hiss than a question.

Colton is barely able to disguise his glee. "There are clues."

"Like what?"

"Your eyes are bloodshot and your hair's messed up."

I impatiently smooth it into place.

"And your tie isn't tied."

I look down. "Shit." I've been so distracted I forgot to tie it, but I do it now.

"I'm guessing the date with Ms. Irish went well." More smirking.

I have a bizarre urge to punch my brother in the face. He's joking, bantering like he always does. But her name has become sacred to me. *It's fucking mine.*

I glare at him with my fists clenched.

Colton laughs and holds up his palms. "Dude. Okay. Chill."

"What happened?" Cash asks.

I don't answer. Trying to explain what *happened* would be like trying to explain the Theory of Relativity to a three-year-old. But, actually, all three of my brothers probably have a clue as to how I'm feeling right about now. Because they've all been through it.

"You can't just give us zero details," Colton protests. "We're invested."

I debate downplaying it, finally settling on, "It went well."

Colton's eyebrows lift. "How well?"

"*Very* well."

"Hallelujah, he finally got laid," Colton rejoices.

I take a step toward him and he darts around the table, dodging me. "I'm *happy* for you, bro. And you're welcome, for your favorite brother's intervention."

"Don't force me to rearrange your face, Colton."

"I'm surprised your mood hasn't improved," he laughs. "Did she look as good as her photo?"

A vision of her on the bed, her flaxen hair cascading in waves over the pillow, her eyes so blue and her pink mouth swollen from my greedy kisses, takes over my entire brain. "She looked so much better than that."

My brothers exchange a look at the naked longing in my voice.

"She must be something special if you spent the whole weekend with her," Cash says.

"She is." *She really, really is. And now I don't know where she is and I don't even know her real name. How the fuck did I let that happen?*

"No wonder you don't want to be here," Colton grins. "I bet she's waiting for you at your apartment right now."

"If she was, I wouldn't be here right now."

Colton laughs knowingly. I throw a pen at his head, which he catches. He's well practiced at this point.

"Can you stop being a complete ass for one minute, Cole? Seriously."

"Unfortunately, he can't," Cash answers for him. "It's not in his nature."

The comment doesn't even land on Colton. "When are you seeing her again?"

"Soon."

Fucking Colton pounces abruptly on my lack of specifics. "You haven't made any plans?"

I rake a hand through my hair.

Which Colton reads correctly as third degree angst. Unfortunately for me, my brothers know me very well. "Don't tell me you didn't get her real name."

Cash groans. "Oh, fuck. You idiot." The same thing happened to him, when he met Dusty. They met at a beach bar in Hawaii, gave each other nicknames, had the best night of their lives together but when he woke up the next morning she was gone. He spent months looking for her before she turned up as our newest junior analyst—which in his case, turned out to be the luckiest coincidence of his life. "I thought you would have learned from my mistake."

"I should have," I admit. "I didn't think she'd leave without saying goodbye this morning." My fucking brothers always get the information out of me, whether I want them to or not. "I've got her number though."

"Then *call* her." Colton gives me a *duh* look.

"I have. Several times. She's not picking up. She has a busy day at work ahead of her. She's probably in a meeting."

"If you need to track her down," Colton says, "get Jake in IT to trace her phone location."

"Don't you have a million girls lighting up your phone incessantly?" Cash takes a seat at the head of the table. "I'm sure she'll answer."

A few days ago I might have appreciated the observation. Right now it only makes things worse. *I don't want them. I want her. And why isn't she answering my calls?*

Cash starts leafing through some paperwork. "Noah, you were obviously busy over the weekend, but I tried to call you a dozen times, to brief you on the meeting this morning. The CEO of Ashton Holdings will be here any minute. Her name is L. Emerson Ashton. You'll just have to wing it. But you've done all the homework so it should be fairly straightforward."

"Her?" Colton helps himself to a donut from the buffet table that's been laid out.

Some little inkling of a sixth sense tweaks somewhere behind my brain.

She works in finance.

She has a high-powered job.

Her father had a lot of heavy expectations.

He recently died.

But L. Emerson Ashton doesn't ring any bells beyond the Ashton Holdings' spreadsheets. *Unless…*

Surely not.

"Yes." Cash confirms. "L. Emerson is a woman. I spoke to her last week. She sounded young. She wasn't happy with the number I gave her. She said Abundance had also made an offer."

I walk over and grab a coffee cup. "A much lower one, I have no doubt. There's no way they offered more than fifteen. Probably more like ten. If anything, we should go lower. We're not fucking budging on fifteen. There's not a snowball's chance in hell that company is worth even close to that much. Not at the moment, at least."

I'm pouring myself a cup of coffee, my back to the door as I rant.

Cash says something.

That's when I hear another voice. *A voice I'd know anywhere. The sweetest voice in the world.* "Hi, I'm Lucky Ashton."

What?

I turn.

Holy fuck.

She's wearing a little black dress. Her hair is smoothed back and clipped on the sides, but the flaxen curls are as wild as ever, spilling over her shoulders.

She's achingly, devastatingly gorgeous.

I love her.

L. Emerson Ashton is *my* Lucky Irish.

27

Lucky

One hour earlier

I CRY all the way through my shower. Real, fat, salty tears that have been accumulating behind some fortified psychological floodgate for nineteen years.

Damn you, Noah Steel. For blowing the lid off some deep emotional well I've been able to keep sealed all this time.

I don't how he did that.

With those filthy-sweet words, that gigantic cock and all those stellar orgasms, that's how.

I wish he was here. I wish I was soaping up those washboard abs, sliding my hand lower, fisting his—

Stop. This isn't helping.

After a while, my tears finally dry up. I rinse my hair and my face, turn the shower off and reach for a towel.

Weirdly, I feel better. Lighter. Freer. Like some of the

existential weight I've been carrying around with me for a long time has lifted.

I check the time. 9:13.

I choose a simple black dress. I brush my hair and leave it loose. But then I think better of it, smoothing it back from my face and clipping it into place with a tortoise-shell barrette on each side. That will have to do, since I don't have time to tame it this morning.

Who am I trying to please anyway? Cash Maddox can kiss my ass. I'm hardly going to make an effort for the shark who's trying to eat my company.

I put on my usual mascara and lip gloss. I notice then that I've got several hickies on my neck that aren't at all subtle.

Really, Steel? What were you trying to do, mark me as your own?

I already know the answer to that question. A small curl of pleasure flutters through me as my body remembers. I put some concealer over the bruises but it doesn't do much to hide them.

My sapphire bracelet catches the light. I try to take it off but the clasp seems stuck. I finally give up and leave it on. *Why, Noah?* It doesn't make sense. Grace must have made a mistake. Two months of studying gems hardly makes her an expert. Machines make gems these days, maybe it's getting harder to tell. I'm sure there are plenty of jewelry stores that use blue boxes.

I pull on some knee-length boots, find my bag and

grab my phone. It's fully charged. There are now fourteen missed calls from the Unknown Caller. And one text.

CALL ME BACK ~ N

I will. But not now. I need all my wits and I'm barely holding it together as it is.

I can hear the shower in Grace's bathroom running, so I quickly text her.

Pray for me. Love you, G. See you tonight

I ride the elevator down to the lobby, take a minute to say hi to the concierge and to stop to smell the flowers in today's bouquet. My mother used to say it was good luck to stop and smell the roses.

If there was ever a day I needed luck, Mama, this is it. Send me a little extra from wherever you are up there. I miss you. Daddy, I'll do the best I can.

Then I grab a cab to the Fifth Avenue address of Invested Enterprises.

On the way, I try to channel my inner calm. After the emotional release of my crying jag, I do feel calmer. I'll negotiate with Cash Maddox and his mulish CFO with all the self-confidence I have—which isn't record-breaking but it's also not nothing. I do happen to be good at my job. I've been studying these numbers my whole life.

There *is* value in Ashton Holdings. And there's huge potential for growth. I just have to convince them of that.

The cab pulls up to the curb. I pay the guy and step out onto the street.

I look up.

I happen to know Invested Enterprises owns the entire skyscraper.

Wow.

It's an impressive building.

Let's do this, L. Emerson.

I take a deep breath. And I step inside.

The lobby is black marble, gold and glass. There's a front desk and a metal-detector entranceway that leads deeper into the lobby, to the area where the rows of elevators are.

"Good morning," the girl at the desk greets me. She's young, gorgeous, very professional and has the whitest teeth I've ever seen. She could be a Dallas Cowboys cheerleader or a Victoria's Secret runway model. It's well publicized that all the brightest new graduates from all over the country flock to apply for jobs at Invested Enterprises. It's the trendiest company to work for in New York.

"Hi. I'm Lucky Ashton. I'm here to meet with Cash Maddox."

She checks the computer. "I have an L. Emerson Ashton at ten."

"Yes, that's me."

"Welcome, Ms. Ashton. Your meeting is on the eighteenth floor. It's Boardroom 1810. Take one of the elevators on the left. When you get to the eighteenth floor, take a right. It's the largest meeting room, at the end of the hall. You can't miss it. They're all waiting for you."

All? My heart is beating fast. The clock on the wall reads 10:01. "Thank you."

A group of young, fashionably-dressed employees who might have just come from a Vogue photoshoot follow me through the metal detector. Talking animatedly, they all wander into elevators on the right. I'm the only one waiting for the elevators on the left.

One opens. I step inside and press 18.

It barely even feels like I'm moving.

If I lose everything, I'll look for a job in Ireland, that's what I'll do. Fuck it all. I'll pack my bags and live a completely different life. I'll rent a little studio apartment with a futon for a bed and a desk that looks out the window over green fields. I'll start over again. So what if I don't have a penny to my name. Or a home. Or possessions. Or a job. At least I'll be free.

Of course I'll call Noah back. Maybe we can even have another weekend together before I fly out.

My stomach does a weird swoop that has nothing to do with the elevator. It has everything to do with the reminder of my spur-of-the-moment trip to Ireland and the reason I was going to do that.

Oh. My. GOD. I forgot to take my pill. I always take it before bed. But on Friday night I was so preoccupied I completely forgot. I FORGOT TO TAKE MY BIRTH CONTROL PILL. I didn't take one on Saturday either. Or Sunday. I FORGOT FOR THREE WHOLE DAYS.

What I *did* do on Friday, Saturday *and* Sunday was have a very unprotected and extremely uninhibited sex-a-thon.

DOES MISSING YOUR PILLS FOR THREE DAYS MEAN YOU CAN…?

Holy shit. I need to google it. I need to get a Plan B. I need to figure out what to do.

The elevator pings and the doors slide open.

I almost don't step out.

Should I rush home and immediately take a pill? All three? Would that make a difference?

The elevators doors start to close and I quickly push the button to keep them open.

What if I'm…

And homeless?

Good work, L. Emerson. Well done. Knocked up, broke and living destitute on the streets. Fantastic use of real world common sense. Way to go, girl.

But there's another tiny part of me—the crazy, impractical part—that doesn't hate the idea. It *is* one of my wildest dreams, after all.

Did some corner of my psyche make me forget on purpose? Did my inner sex goddess and her Earth Mother twin sabotage me? You bitches! This is not what I need right now!

I need to get my shit together and get to this meeting. I'm still holding the button that keeps the doors open.

I take a deep breath, square my shoulders and step out of this elevator. But I feel dazed, my head full of visions of me living under a bridge with a hungry baby.

What would Noah do if I was? He was definitely enthusiastic about not using condoms.

On autopilot, I take a right and start walking down the hall to the only room with an open door, glass walls and, even from here, expansive views of the city skyline.

There's a tall man standing near the door. And a second one. I can see another man with his back turned. He's talking. Gruffly. His voice is loud enough for me to hear what he's saying. "There's no way they offered more than fifteen. Probably more like ten. If anything, we should go lower. We're not fucking budging on fifteen. There's not a snowball's chance in hell that company is worth even close to that much."

His voice sounds almost sounds familiar. But no, it's more aggressive. More pissed off and cut-throat.

I get to the doorway and the two men closest to the door turn.

They're both big, wide-shouldered and dark-haired. One is slightly taller, more stern and seasoned-looking. The other one has a more laid-back vibe and can't quite contain his amusement. They're both absurdly good-looking men.

God. Why do they look almost familiar?

The taller one steps forward and holds out his hand. "Cash Maddox."

I shake it, just like my father taught me to. Firm but not too firm and keep it brief. "Hi, I'm Lucky Ashton."

"This is my brother Colton, COO," Cash is saying. It's then that the third man turns. "And that's Noah, my CFO."

You've got to be kidding me.

Holy shit.

No.

No no no *no no* NO.

It's him.

My Noah.

None other than the man I spent the entire weekend in bed with, doing shockingly intimate things, and now there's a very small chance—okay, maybe not *very* small— that he may have actually impregnated me.

This can't be happening.

Oh, it's happening all right.

He looks different in this setting. More serious. *That suit fits him in a way that should be illegal.* Meaner. More intimidating. But no less handsome.

His brothers are hot, gorgeous men, but they don't have that sexy teddy bear thing going on that Noah has.

Except that he's lost the best parts of his teddy-bear-ness in this setting. He's more grizzly-on-the-prowl.

I hate him. I hate how fucking beautiful he is. I hate that he and his arrogant billionaire brothers have all the power in this situation and I have exactly none.

My to-die-for lover is the evil CFO.

He's the one who's going to ruin me.

Noah Steel is Noah Fucking Maddox.

28

WE STAND THERE SORT OF FACING off, both of us too shocked to speak.

Even though I'm speechless, my brain is still able to replay a series of sex-flashbacks that might make me blush if I wasn't so pissed off. *The hot throb of his spilling cock as he came so hard I was overflowing with it, my body squeezing his in clenching, pleasure-heavy pulls.*

It's hard to reconcile that my beautiful lover is the same man who's about to ruin my life.

I heard what he was saying as I walked in the door. *We're not fucking budging on fifteen. There's not a snowball's chance in hell that company is worth even close to that much.*

He's wrong.

It *is* worth that much. Much more than that. Or it *could* be if I only had enough time to get it there.

It's very possible that I'm good enough at my job to

do that. Sure, it's also possible that I'm not. If my decrepit old man Board is any judge, I'm not up to the task. But deep down I know I am.

"Wait a minute." It's the brother Cash introduced as Colton. His gaze is on Noah, who's still staring at me in mute shock and stunned disbelief. Then it slides over to me. "*Lucky* Ashton? The L. of L. Emerson Ashton stands for *Lucky*?"

"Yes," I confirm.

It doesn't take a PhD to figure out that Colton is the brother who set Noah up on our blind date. I know the story. And he knows at least half my alias, which might as well be the whole thing. It's easy to see that Colton understands what's going on here—and why his brother looks like he's just seen a ghost.

Noah finally speaks. "Lucky—"

At exactly the same time, Colton bursts into raucous laughter. "Ho-o-ly shit."

"What?" Cash asks, still in the dark.

"Looks like we've got ourselves a little bit of a snafu with your latest deal, bro." Colton seems to find this hilarious.

I don't know if it's the overload of emotion I've experienced over the past 72 hours that's making me feel madder than hell. I fell in love this weekend, it's as simple and life-changing as that. To realize that I've fallen in love with an asshole sort of breaks my heart in slow motion as I'm standing here glaring at these three ultra-powerful, loaded-beyond-belief, kings-of-New-York brothers who eat people like me for breakfast and spit out their bones without a second thought.

That's why they're at the top of the heap. Because they don't care about anyone but themselves. Obviously. Because they—and especially *him*, the CFO with no heart —would like nothing more than to steal my father's company right out from under me.

I decide in the moment that I'd rather go bankrupt than take their fifteen million of pity money. Actually, it's not even pity. Just hard-ball greed. They know they're getting a bargain and they couldn't care less about how much it's going to hurt me.

At least with bankruptcy you don't *owe* anything once you've declared it. So what if you can't borrow, your credit's shot and banks won't even look at you for a decade. The upside is that you don't have to pay back high-interest loans for years to come. At this point I'll take it.

Maybe the Irish banks won't have that information. Maybe they won't care. I'll have to renew the old passport my mother had issued for our trip when I was three that I've let lapse. I'll start a new life.

Me and my little blue-eyed baby.

I don't wait for Colton to explain to Cash what the situation is. "I came here to negotiate." My voice sounds cold. I'm looking right at Noah when I say it. "Since your CFO has very clearly stated that you're not willing to budge on fifteen, then there's nothing to discuss. Because that number doesn't work for me." I turn to Cash. "Thank you for your time. There's no need for me to take any more of it. The deal's off."

Before I burst into tears—my new thing that I have no idea how to control—I walk out.

29

Just as I reach the elevators, I hear footsteps behind me.

"Lucky—"

"Leave me alone." The elevator doors slide open and I step inside. "I have nothing to say to you."

"Bullshit." Noah steps in beside me.

So I step back out again. "I'll take the stairs, then, if you insist."

"We're on the eighteenth floor."

"Then I guess I've got a long walk."

Noah sighs heavily, like I'm testing his patience. *Jerk! He's* testing *my* patience! "Fine," he growls. "You take the elevator then."

He's holding the door, to keep it open.

Glaring at him, I step back into the elevator.

He removes his hand and the doors start to close. Just before they close all the way, he slides through.

"You—!" *Oh my god!* Now I'm trapped in here with him.

"Lucky, we need to talk about this."

I almost punch the door-open button again but I don't want to play his games. So I punch the button for the lobby impatiently until the elevator starts to move. At least I think it's moving. Like everything in this building, it's so swish and modern I can't actually tell. "I already told you, I have nothing to say to you."

"Irish—"

"Don't call me that," I snap.

With infinite patience that pisses me off: "Lucky. I couldn't have known the company we were trying to buy was yours."

"That doesn't change who you are. A bully, that's what you are. An evil bully who doesn't care about anyone but yourself."

He exhales a laugh. *The asshole!*

"You think this is *funny*?" I seethe.

"Not at all, baby girl."

"Do *not* call me that." I swear if I could shoot daggers out of my eyeballs right now, I would. Mercifully, the ride is vertigo-inducingly swift. The elevator doors slide open and I stride out, making a beeline for the front door.

Noah easily keeps up with me, returning a few greetings of gorgeous, glamorous-looking people who obviously adore and respect him as we walk through the busy, ultra-luxurious lobby.

Of course it's luxurious. Because he's siphoning money out of every struggling company in New York and straight into his own bank account.

I march out onto the street to wave down a taxi, wildly annoyed that he's still standing right next to me. "Lucky. This is my car. My driver. Let me take you home or to your office or wherever you're going and we can talk this through."

"We can talk it through right here. You and your shark brothers made an offer for my company that was too low. I rejected it. There. We've talked it through." A cab pulls up and I open the door, sliding in.

Noah slides in next to me, actually lifting me up to carefully place me further along so he can get in. *Why does he have to be so fucking big and built?*

"What part of leave me alone don't you understand?" I ask icily.

"Where to?" the driver asks, oblivious to the tension going on in the back seat.

I think about getting out of the cab and trying for another one but I know he'll just follow me.

My eyes are blazing.

We sit there for a few seconds.

I'm stalling, because I don't want to say the address. Then he'll know where I live.

Noah gives the taxi driver my home address.

"Sure thing, Chief," the driver replies, pulling into traffic.

Right. Of course the evil CFO has thoroughly done his due diligence and knows everything about me, my business and my home. Every gory detail of my life has bled all over those spreadsheets and paperwork he's no doubt been poring over for weeks. I cringe when I think about all that red ink, which might as well be printed in my own blood.

I scooch all the way over to the door on my side, ignoring him. He can dominate me in the bedroom of our dreamy, one-off, unrealistic little bubble all he wants, but not in the boardroom. And not out here in the real world.

As if I'm not furious enough, he keeps glancing over at me with actual concern and an inkling of amusement. Like he feels for me. Like he's *not* my heartless arch nemesis who's in the process of unfeelingly destroying me.

The cab pulls up in front of my building and Noah hands the driver a hundred dollar bill.

Fine. He can pay for it. He can fucking afford it, no doubt about that.

I get out of the cab while he's paying and hurry to try to find my fob that opens the front door of my building.

But he's already there. *Damn it!*

"I can ask the front desk to call security, you know," I tell him. "There's no way in hell I'm letting you into my apartment."

"Lucky. You've got this all wrong."

"All *wrong*? Actually, you made everything crystal clear,

Mr. Maddox. I didn't have any difficulty whatsoever understanding the terms of your offer." My hands are fisted on my hips. "You think you're a big shot who knows everything and controls everyone, but you're not. And you don't."

The bastard has the nerve to bite back an empathetic smile. "I never said I control anyone."

"You act like you do."

"Lucky. Invested Enterprises' offer is off the table, we agree on that. No harm done."

"No harm *done*? That's easy for *you* to say. Your life isn't imploding!"

"Let me come up. I want to make sure you're okay."

"No! You're the reason I'm *not* okay! How can I be *okay* when you're pulling out all the stops to devalue and destroy my livelihood and dismantle my father's legacy?" I fully understand that it's not Noah's, Cash's or anyone else's fault that I'm in the position I'm in. It's my father's fault. His legacy is a crumbling empire with a mountain of debt. Still, Noah's the one standing here and I need to take out my frustration on *someone*. It's true he's made my day a whole lot worse. *Because I fucking fell in love with him and everything about this hurts.* "Since when do you care if *anyone* is okay?"

"I'm not trying to devalue anything. It's just business. A business I did not know was associated with *your* livelihood or *your* father's legacy."

"But you knew it was *someone's*! That's just as bad! It's evil!"

He gives me a look. "Shrewd, yes. Seeking out opportunities that will make a profit, definitely. I think 'evil' is overstating it. It's all part of making deals. You know that."

"Well, *I* don't make deals with the devil!" Maybe I'm overreacting but I don't care. "Stop following me. Stay here. Do *not* follow me."

"Let me come up."

"No! Absolutely not."

I can read his thoughts as he stares down at me with that sincerity I used to love about him. Now I hate it. *Always say yes.* Saying yes to this man has brought me nothing but trouble.

His voice is annoyingly smooth and deep, with that smoky husk that used to turn me on. "I'm Noah, remember? The one who can talk you off a ledge and always saves the day."

I let out a scoffing laugh. "You haven't saved anyone's day today. Except maybe your own." I almost call him *Steel.* But of course that was just a mask.

I hate how much I miss *that* Noah. *My* Noah. I miss the haven of his comfort. I miss laughing with him. I miss our corny nicknames. I miss how good he made me feel.

How can a single weekend with a total stranger feature so many of the best memories of my life?

But that was just an illusion, of course.

"Actually," he says, "my day isn't going well at all." There's regret in him. Maybe even sadness.

Which, if I stay here, might actually sway me. "Well, that can sometimes happen when you set out to destroy other people's lives. See you around, Maddox."

I turn to leave but he grabs my hand. "Lucky. Stop overreacting. I'm not leaving you like this. I didn't *know* it was *your* company. You can't hold that against me. The offer we made for Ashton Holdings was a fair one, considering its value in the current market. We're trying to run a profitable business, just like you are."

"By forcing smaller companies to fold under your billionaire behemoth pressure?"

His blue eyes do that fucking sparkling thing. "No one's *forcing* you to do anything. It was an *offer*, nothing more. And a more generous one than the other offer you got. What did Abundance offer you? Ten? Twelve? Are you holding a grudge against fucking Chad too?"

He makes it sound like I'm being petty and unreasonable. "No," I grumble petulantly.

"Then why are you so mad at me?"

This is going to make me sound even more petty and petulant, but I say it anyway. Because it's true. "You didn't have to be so mean about it."

"Mean?" Like the word is foreign to him.

"Yes. Mean." I mimic his deep voice. "'We're not fucking budging on fifteen. There's not a snowball's chance in hell that company is worth even close to that much'. You *know* it's worth that much! You know it's potentially worth five times that much!"

"I know it is."

I glare at him. "You know it is?"

"Of course I do."

"Yet you still undervalued my potential and my father's entire life's work?"

"Lucky, my *job* is to find struggling, undervalued investment companies and make low offers on them."

"Yeah. And you're just so fucking good at your *job*." I don't even know what I'm accusing him of at this point. When he explains it like that it almost sounds reasonable. But that doesn't change the fact that their too-low offer is now off the table and I'm back to square one. "Does being that grumpy and intimidating usually work for you?"

"I'm not usually *that* grumpy. I was in a fucking bad mood this morning. You know why? Because the little Irish minx who rocked my world all weekend was gone when I woke up this morning. *You* walked out on *me. I* should be the one who's mad."

We're standing out on the street having a full-blown argument. People glance at us as they step around us. "I didn't walk out on you. I didn't want to wake you up! And I *did* have a busy day. I was nervous about the meeting with your brother and his famously bull-headed CFO! It takes all my focus these days to keep my world from crumbling underneath me. Which of course *you* wouldn't understand at all! I needed some time to myself. Not that it helped." I add, in my own defense, "Anyway, I left my number. You can delete it now."

"That's not happening. I called it. Twenty fucking times. Actually, more. You didn't bother answering."

"Like I said, I was trying to psych myself up for the hellish meeting I was about to go to. Which turned out to be a lot more hellish than I ever imagined. Because of you."

Do not cry. Do not cry.

The tears are stinging behind my eyes. Noah's expression is so concerned and so full of care it makes this whole thing ten times worse.

I pull away from him. "I have to go. Goodbye."

I hate the sound of the word like I've never hated anything.

30

NOAH

"Goodbye, my ass, Irish."

She glares at me with eyes so soulful it makes my chest hurt. Then she turns away and storms into her building. I follow her inside.

I'm ready for whatever she gives me. If she calls security I'll wait out on the street for her to come out again. She has to eventually.

If I can get to her floor and she refuses to let me into her apartment I'll order a pizza or something until she gets annoyed by my knocking and lets me in, even if it takes all day. Or all week. I'll call a fucking camping store and get them to deliver one of those camper beds. I'll live out in her hallway until she believes me. I'm a goddamn billionaire, I'll figure it out.

A billionaire who's spent my whole life making money, relentlessly, at the cost of having a life.

I don't want to do that anymore. I want to *spend* some fucking money for once. On her.

I refuse to walk away. Not for this reason. If she decides she hates me for other reasons…no. I still won't walk away.

I've waited too long for her. I've spent too many nights alone, wondering if I'll ever find that one perfect, elusive girl who's meant for me and only me.

Now that I've found her, the last fucking thing I'd do is to let her walk away, especially like this. It would hurt far more than anything else ever could.

If she hates me now, then I'll prove her wrong. I don't care what it takes. I don't care what it costs me. She's worth all of it.

She looked so scared and alone when she walked into our boardroom, putting on the bravest face. The three—and sometimes four—of us can be intimidating. We were once described in some article as "a united front of hot, powerful alpha billionaires" and it's true that we more often than not get our way because of it. She didn't back down to any one of us and that takes some fucking grit.

I was stunned to see her there. Of course I was. I was even more stunned by how fucking beautiful she is. I'd gotten used to it in the peacefulness of our hotel room. The whole weekend was like a dream I never wanted to wake up from.

But seeing her under the harsh lights of reality—so soft-looking, so sun-lit, so exquisitely perfect, like an angel or a goddess who happened to drop into the realm of us mere mortals to humor our mundanity for an hour or two, blinding me with her beauty…*I knew.*

I already knew. I already fucking *knew.* If she struck me with Cupid's arrow over the weekend, she impaled me through the goddamn heart this morning, so deeply and irrevocably that if she decides to pull it out again, I'll bleed out all over the floor. It'll kill me.

We're in her elevator now. She's still frowning at me and she's so fucking cute all I want to do is get on my knees and grovel.

"I don't know why you're following me," she huffs. "It's trespassing at this point."

"Not if you invite me in."

"That tracks. You're a vampire, after all. Feeding on the dreams of people like me."

"I like the melodrama you're infusing into our romance, Irish. I'd say it's more Brontë than Dickens though. I'll pace out on the street like Heathcliff, pining for you moodily in a black cloak if it'll help."

"'Help' is irrelevant at this point. Nothing's going to *help*. Our 'romance'"—in air quotes— "ended when you devalued my company—very aggressively, I might add— and you *knew* you were devaluing it! Which makes it so much worse. That company is *important* to me. It's important to all the people who rely on it for their salary and to pay their mortgages and to invest in their children's futures. These deals *affect* people. But of course none of that matters to someone like you."

She really is in a mood, but fair enough. She's stressed out and no wonder. She *is* about to lose everything. Her options are very limited, that was painfully clear in the paperwork. She was relying on an offer from us that might save her. *If only I'd known.* But I know now. And I'm about to do a lot more than save her. Because if she doesn't let me, I'll fucking drown. "You're right."

More glaring.

"I didn't think about how our offer would make the CEO of Ashton Holdings feel."

"Obviously."

"I'm going to make a new offer. Not through Invested Enterprises, but personally."

"Don't bother. It's too late. I'm not interested in anything you have to offer."

"It's not too late, Irish."

"It *is* too late." A tear pools and she quickly wipes it away. It's something I simply can't handle. My heart literally aches, like she's tugging on that big-ass arrow she stuck in there. Nothing in the world matters to me except making this right. "I hate you," she whispers.

I can't stop myself from saying it. I'm feeling it too hard. "Well, I *love* you, so there."

31

Lucky

"As ɪꜰ." I unlock my door and open it, but only a crack. I stand in front of it, so he can't barge in. "You can't."

"The fuck I can't."

God, the man is infuriating. "You don't even know me."

I don't want to invite him in. More accurately, I don't want to invite Noah Maddox in. I only want Noah Steel. But he doesn't exist.

"I *do* know you," he insists. "In many ways, better than anyone ever has. I'm the only one who knows what you sound like when you—"

"Stop." I know what he's going to say and I don't want to be reminded of any of that. And I hate that he's right. The problem is, it doesn't matter. "Anyway, thanks, I guess, for escorting me home against my will. I hope you have a wonderful day ruining lives and adding to your vault of money. Oh—" I hold out my wrist where the sapphire bracelet circles. "I can't get this off but if you could please take it off for me you can have it back. I don't want it."

Noah doesn't take the bracelet off. Instead, he gets down on his knees, sliding his warm palms around the backs of my bare thighs as though to keep me here.

"Lucky Emerson O'Callahan from County Cork Irish Ashton, don't fucking leave me. I'm sorry. I'm sorry my brothers and I tried to buy your company. I'm sorry I didn't realize it was yours. I'm sorry we offered you fair but low market value even though the company clearly has huge potential for growth. I'm sorry I said we wouldn't fucking budge on fifteen million in a mean way. I'm sorry you had a stressful day today and it was my fault. I'm sorry I couldn't take some of that worry away this morning before you snuck out on me. I'm sorry I didn't get a chance to kiss you and make sweet love to you until you were happy again, which is all I really want to do. I'm sorry we didn't tell each other the truth about who we were. But I'm also not sorry about that, because then you would have hated me before our weekend ended and that would have ripped my heart right out of my chest. I'm sorry your life has been so hard, for a long time. I'm sorry you lost your parents and you've spent so much time feeling so alone. I'm sorry you've been scared that you're going to lose your company and your apartment. And that *would* be *very* fucking scary. I'm sorry you think I'm evil. I'm not evil, I promise, and I'm going to prove that to you no matter how long that takes. I'm sorry you don't believe I've already fallen for you. *Hard.* I fell in love with you the minute I saw you and every minute of our weekend together only made me fall harder. And then I fell even more in love with you today and I'm falling even more in love with you right now. It just keeps compounding on itself exponentially. The thing is, I've *also* been alone for a long time. I have my brothers but I'm not talking about that kind of alone. I mean *alone* alone. I mean the kind of alone where you feel lost and sort of broken because you know you're fucking destined to love someone with everything you've got, but you can't *find* that person. So you spend all your time just fucking *looking* for her. And you start to doubt everything about life itself. Because there's always this big black hole in the middle of everything and you don't know how to fill it. The thing is, Irish, you filled it. You just waltzed into that restaurant the other night and fucking *filled* it. With your white-gold hair and your blue eyes and that way you look at me like you're exasperated with me. *Gone.* And don't tell me I can't know that. Don't tell me it's too soon. I know what a fucking black hole feels like, Lucky Irish. I also, now, because of you, know what it feels like to have it filled up. Because suddenly there you were."

32

I'M LITERALLY SPEECHLESS.

"I'm going to prove to you that I'm not evil, baby girl. Starting now," Noah says. "I know I have to prove myself to you, and I will. Do you have a pen and some paper?"

I'm still kind of reeling from his speech, which included at least a dozen of the nicest and most romantic things anyone has ever said to me in my entire life. All I'm carrying is my small bag that contains my phone. "Um… not on me."

He gives me a look. And flicks his eyebrows. Toward my apartment. "Inside?"

"Probably."

"I need to write something down."

His gush was kind of life-changing. I can already tell I'll never forget it. But it still doesn't change my situation, my discovery about who he is or all that has happened over the last hour. I don't want to invite him in. Because if he continues to be this nice, apologetic, *hot*, perceptive *and* grovelly, I know exactly what will happen. "I'll go get one for you. You wait here."

"I need a table too. To write on." When I don't immediately invite him in, he adds, "I promise I'll leave as soon as I've written it down."

"What do you have to write?"

"I'll tell you *as* I'm writing it."

Against *all* my better judgement I push the door open, gently extricate myself from his grip and walk inside, leaving it open behind me.

My apartment, as always, looks stunning and inviting in the mid-morning light. Rays of sunlight land idyllically on the quaint, plush window seat and the etched-glass orb lamp I bought from an antique store in Vermont one weekend when Grace and I randomly decided to rent a car (she knows how to drive) and spent a weekend at an Airbnb she found on the shores of Lake Champlain. It was only a few weeks before my father died and my life turned upside down. I don't know why, but I always leave the lamp on.

Beyond the window seat, outside on the balcony, my flowering indigo wisteria that climbs along the edging so it frames the whole view, looks cheerful, blissfully unaware it's about to be pulled out by its roots.

A lot of people who visit my apartment comment that it looks like a decorating magazine spread and I consider that now, as Noah sees it for the first time. It looks so beautiful and cozy it breaks my jaded heart.

"Wow." There's that manly sincerity again. "This is a nice apartment."

Which reminds me why I actually hate him and why I can't let my guard down with him, no matter how beautiful and heartfelt his little soliloquies might be. "Thanks. Too bad I'll be being dragged out by repo men by the end of the month." My surly melodramatics might be a *tad* overdone, but I forgive myself since the occasion does actually call for it.

A smirk plays at the corners of his annoyingly perfect mouth, like he finds my angst adorable. "The pen and paper, please?"

I go to the closet where I keep my office supplies. I hand him a pen and a few sheets of paper.

Noah motions toward one of my kitchen stools. "May I?"

"Help yourself." I put on the kettle. "You want some peppermint tea?"

"Okay. Where's your roommate?"

"She has a really busy schedule on Mondays. She won't be back until late. That is, if she comes back at all tonight. She might end up staying with her new boyfriend."

"The one she met through the app?"

"Yes." I don't want to talk about the app. "Can we

make this quick? I need to go to work." *And figure out how to start filing for bankruptcy.*

Noah sits and starts scrawling something. "I have my own business entity that's separate from Invested Enterprises. It's called Blue Sky Enterprises. I am the sole founder and director. I use it for real estate investments and a few other business investments."

"Good for you." I realize I'm being surly but I have to. I need this barrier up. *Way* up. Because his muscles are straining even under his suit porn. His size and his outrageous in-your-face masculinity are sort of filling up the room and infusing it with those crazy pheromones he emits.

He smells so fucking good.

That damn leather and woodsmoke scent reminds me of…*sucking on him. Swallowing in lusty mouthfuls.*

He's busy writing so I can watch him without him noticing. His hair is too long, curling behind his ears and down the back of his sun-tanned neck in little flicks. *It was so thick when I grabbed handfuls of it, when he was licking me and eating me so greedily. I came so incredibly hard.* "So this offer has nothing to do with Invested Enterprises, Cash, Colton or anyone else."

"I told you, I'm not interested in your offer." Irritably. I add tea bags and pour boiling water into two mugs. I slide one over to him then lean against the counter. Holding my tea in both hands, I blow on it.

Noah starts reading to me. "'Blue Sky Enterprises

puts forth the offer of fifty million dollars for one percent ownership of Ashton Holdings.'"

"What?" I laugh but there's no humor in it. "Don't you mean *fifteen*? One percent? Is this a joke? Why are you even bringing this up again? We've agreed the whole thing is off the table."

"This is a different offer. Obviously." He continues reading. "'L. Emerson Ashton will remain in place as CEO of Ashton Holdings. If, at some point in the future she chooses to name a co-CEO and/or a successor, those appointments will be solely at her discretion, with appropriate approval from the Ashton Holdings' Board of Directors. It is agreed by both parties that Noah Maddox will be employed by Ashton Holdings as a CEO's consultant for an annual salary of one dollar.'"

Is this some kind of game he's playing? I don't understand it. He's saying crazy things. Is he trying to smash my heart to smithereens? I take a sip of my tea. It's too hot. So I set it back on the counter. "Noah," I whisper, because it's the only volume I can summon right now. "I think you should leave."

He sets down the pen. He stands up and comes over to me. Very easily and very carefully, he lifts me and sets me on the counter. Slowly, he pushes my knees apart and stands between them. His warm palm slides under my hair and around the nape of my neck, lightly squeezing. Just like he did when we were in the restaurant. My body remembers even if my emotions are in shambles. "I wasn't lying when I said it's my mission now to make every single one of those wildest dreams come true, Irish."

"You can't—" He stops me, putting a finger over my lips.

"At its most valuable, Ashton Holdings was worth seventy-four million dollars, give or take. The decisions you've made over the past six months have been good ones, Lucky. If you stay that course and make a couple of tweaks that I can help you with, I predict the company will rebound to at least that much within the next two years. Within the next four, I think we could triple that number. I'm not trying to mess with you and I'm definitely not trying to buy you. I'm making a legitimate investment."

"At *one percent*?" It's been too much of a morning. And a weekend. And a year. I can't get my head around it.

"The other ninety-nine will belong to you and all those magical babies you're planning on having. I've heard the magic ones are more expensive."

33

OH MY GOD. That reminds me.

The things he's saying to me aren't fully absorbing. It's too much to hope for. It's too much to accept.

But at the mention of magical babies, my very urgent issue comes roaring back into the spotlight.

Since there's little to no chance Noah will leave if I ask him to and since I *really* need to figure out what to do, I blurt it out. After all, he's as much a part of this needing-to-google-it-immediately situation as I am. "I forgot to take my pill."

"What pill?"

"*The* pill, Noah. All weekend. It just completely slipped my mind. I remembered right before our meeting this morning. I came home so I could take all three. But I need to find out if that would work."

"Work?" He's silent for a few seconds, until what I'm

explaining to him fully processes. "You mean…you might already be knocked up with my magical baby?"

It's not helping that he keeps describing it like that. It's also not helping that the pure emotion on his face at that exact moment, which I could only describe as uncut joy, makes me fall sort of utterly and distressingly in love with him. Even more than I already was. "I mean…I doubt it could happen that fast."

"It could definitely have happened that fast, Irish. We fucked non-stop."

"God. I *know* we did. But it doesn't always happen the first time." Even if he is evil—and all signs are pointing to the fact that he very much isn't—he feels too good to push away. Which could be extremely problematic because I've known the man for a grand total of *three days* and my entire life already seems to be insistently winding itself around him like a tenacious super-strength vine with seeking, coiling tendrils that won't take no for an answer. *Almost as though it desperately wants to keep him.*

"What about the second, third, fourth, tenth or fifteenth time?" His question comes out sounding sort of…filthy. Also not helping. Because it's so full of love, lust, sincerity, humor, hotness, carefulness and all the other things I've never seen converged so perfectly in one human being before.

"No wonder I could barely walk this morning."

Despite everything, we both laugh.

He places his warm, strong hands on my bare thighs,

slowly sliding them up. He leans close to whisper in my ear. "Are you wet for me, baby girl?"

I place my hand on his chest. "Noah. This is serious."

"So's my fucking hard-on, Irish. I missed you so much. Don't ever do that again."

"Do what?"

"*Leave.* Always wake me up."

Always. Like we'll have a thousand more mornings.

I suddenly crave those thousand mornings with my whole entire heart.

His fingers slide over my—yes, saturated, because this man has an effect on me I can't control—panties, easing the stretchy lace to the side.

I think about trying to stop him. I *should* stop him. We haven't resolved any of this.

But then his fingers glide over my clit and I forget why I'm mad at him.

I reach for him like some internal motherboard is in control of my actions, rubbing my palm over the front of his pants. *Jesus, he wasn't kidding about his hard-on.* It's only been a few hours but it shocks me all over again how freaking huge he is.

Noah releases himself, kissing me as I grip his hot, thick, *gigantic* cock.

We're both breathing hard, sort of frantic to taste and *feel* each other, like we've both been suffering from withdrawal and need our fix.

Noah guides his cock to my slick pussy, barely pushing

into me. I moan into his mouth because nothing has ever felt so good as Noah Steel—or Maddox—whoever the hell he is, he feels like *mine.*

He doesn't pull back, but he slows down, holding my face to murmur, "So are you going to accept Blue Sky's offer?"

I arch toward him, gripping him, squirming to take more of him. "You couldn't have been a little more creative with the name? Like, maybe Azure Blue Sky Enterprises? Or Periwinkle Blue Sky Enterprises? Maybe you're the one who needs a consultant."

"I'll change the name to whatever the fuck you want it to be if you'll just say yes to me. All you have to do is initial it and I'll get my lawyers to draft it up for our final signatures."

He pushes deeper into me and the stretching burn makes me gasp. "You really have *fifty million dollars* sitting around burning a hole in your pocket?"

"I know you're obsessed with what's in my pocket, Irish." He thrusts all the way in and I moan.

Oh god, I'm about to come. And I can't help it. "Is that fifty million dollars in your pocket or are you just happy to see me?"

We both laugh and the movement rubs against a perfect trigger deep, deep inside me. If he would just do that *one* more time…

I'm writhing on his big cock as he holds me still, like he's prolonging this. He knows I'm on the brink. He's making me wait for it. "And to answer your question, yes. I want to invest in you. In us. I'll spend every penny I have to make you happy, Lucky Irish. I'd let my entire empire crumble to the ground to have you. I know it's fast, I fucking know that. But I *love* you. I love you."

I love you too. Even though it's much too soon and this is happening at lightning speed and I haven't spoken those words since I was three years old. "You can always move to Ireland with me and we can sleep on a futon if we have to." I cry out as his unbelievably thick cock fucks me hard and deep. "This isn't helping me google my question about missing all those pills, Steel," I breathe. "I'm still calling you Steel, by the way. Because a certain part of you feels like a hot, newly-forged pillar of it."

"You mean this one?" He grips my hips and pulls out a little before driving even deeper. He's *so* deep, I get that sense again of being completely possessed by him—that addictive one, where I want him there with all my heart, stuffing me so full of his starry pleasure and his skewering beauty. Changing my life.

"Oh, Noah. Oh god."

"Say yes, little Irish. Stop taking your pills. Accept my offer. Come home with me tonight. Move in with me. Have my magical babies. Say yes."

"Yes. Yes. Yes."

WE END up spending the entire afternoon in my bed.

My bedroom suite is up a small set of stairs in its own nook with two large French-style windows, one in the bedroom and one in my bathroom. Both of them open outward and there's a tall tree with leaves that frame the quirky little water tower on the building next door. So if you ignore the noise of the honking cars down below, you can pretend to be somewhere out in the breezy French countryside instead of right here in the middle of New York City.

My European Summer walls and my decorating choices only enhance the vibe.

It's romantic.

It's even more romantic with a big, warm, well-hung, hair-dusted, sweet-talking and extremely virile sex addict in my bed. The man has crazy stamina and there's *nothing* he won't do, I'm learning. Turns out there's nothing *I* won't do either. I'm new at this so he's careful with me when it becomes too much, but no less thorough. We can't seem to get close enough, or high enough.

If there was nothing else to this, I think I'd still be in love with him just because of all those orgasms. They change you. They make you feel like you have no choice but to fully realize yourself, when all along you doubted you would.

Like you've sprouted wings.

Like your entire being is one big pulsing heartbeat that's perfectly in sync with the pumping twin heartbeat of the brand new love of your life.

Like you'll never be alone again because your body will always remember what it feels like to be made love to in the most sincere, ravenous and soul-touching way.

It's a lot. And it's the best feeling I've ever had by a magnitude of around a quadrillion.

After Noah made me come three times in the kitchen, he asked me again to initial the contract he wrote and I did. He took a photo of it and emailed it to his lawyers and then sent them a few other emails.

Then he carried me up my little staircase and has made me come a total of twelve more times. I counted.

I never knew I could even *get* into the positions he gets me into. All I know is that the man is a beast who hands out life-changing climaxes like Santa hands out presents.

And I've just had four dedicated hours of Christmas morning.

Wrapped in Noah's arms, my limbs feel both heavy and light. I'm so sated I might be floating on a bed of clouds.

After a while he gets up and runs the shower. Then he carries me into it and he lifts me, leans me up against the Italian Celeste tiles and makes love to me again. I have tears in my eyes I come so hard. I'm very sore. I have bruises from his fingers and his mouth. My thighs are streaked with his overflowing cum.

"Hey." Noah sets me down on my feet carefully, tipping my chin up with two fingers so I'm gazing up at him. "I'm sorry. I'm pushing you too hard. I'm just so fucking hot for you, baby. You drive me crazy. I'll slow down."

"It's okay, Noah. I wanted you to. I needed you. Every single time."

It's true. I'm addicted to him. Not just how good he feels but the way he banishes all the fears. All the loneliness. When he's inside me, they're *gone*. Just, *poof*. They're outside somewhere and they can't get in. Because my body, my heart and my soul are so full of *him* and what he gives me. The lust and the pleasure. The spilling, gushing warmth. The fun and the laughter. The searing intimacy and the obsessive connection.

There's simply no room for anything else.

He kisses me softly and washes me like I'm breakable.

Then he turns off the shower and dries me, carrying me into my bedroom. "I'm taking you back to my place. We're going to meet with my lawyer and go through the details."

I've forgiven him, if there was anything to forgive. Either way, I think he might be about to far more than make up for it, if he's true to his word. And he's a Noah—he's *the* Noah—so I'm guessing his word is as good as it gets.

I know now that he has a gruff side. His grizzly bear. But when we're alone, all I get is sex god teddy bear with a sweet-and-filthy mouth. When his grizzly shows its face, like now, it reminds me of the Real World, the one we're about to go back into.

Honestly, I'm kind of tired. "There's no rush."

"We'll have some dinner and we can stay there tonight. If you want to."

I touch his face, brushing my fingers against the stubble on his square jaw, so familiar to me now. I kiss his mouth because it's heartbreakingly perfect.

It's all very overwhelming to think about, the whirl-wind of the past four days. So much has happened, it's hard to chew on the enormity of any one thing, let alone all of it.

I could refuse. Part of me wants to. To sleep for a solid twelve hours, work through some of this stuff ratio-nally and regroup in the morning. But a much more fervent part of me wants to believe him and trust him and be with him for the rest of time. Because I'm starting to suspect that I'd let *my* entire empire—the existential one and the emotional one as well as the business one—burn to the ground just to keep him.

"Lucky?" He lets me kiss him. Then he holds my face and gazes into my eyes. "Please come with me. I'll bring you home later if you want me to. I'll take such good care of you. Say yes."

It's scary as hell to fall this hard and this fast. But it feels so good it's impossible to slow it down or to resist it. So I let my heart lead me. "Okay."

35

I PACK an overnight bag just in case I stay at Noah's, even though I'll probably come home later. The weekend and the day are catching up with me.

I don't allow myself to think about tomorrow. I'll be going back to work to either find a new investor or buyer and/or to start looking into filing for bankruptcy—or I won't.

As for the…*magical baby*…it's still Monday. I can still google it. I can still figure it out. I make a point of fully tuning out L. Emerson's internal tirade that's trumpeting through my subconscious: *Have you completely and totally lost your mind????* And also the Earth Mother/sex goddess team, who are clutching at hope and doing high fives. *No need for that trip to Ireland after all!!*

Noah's business offer still doesn't seem real. I take a

deep breath, putting it—along with the long list of other things I'll worry about later—out of my mind as we make our way onto the street, his arm firmly around me and his hand holding mine.

There's a fancy-looking but understated car waiting in front of my building. As soon as the driver sees Noah, he opens the back door for us.

Noah helps me get in. I slide along the back seat and he gets in next to me. The scene reminds me of our taxi ride earlier this morning. We had a fight. Then we sort of made up. Then he made an insane offer to buy my company. Then we had outrageously passionate make-up sex that changed the entire alchemy of my soul, like we're now irrevocably bonded in a way that can't be undone.

The seats are made of thick leather that could actually be Italian. Everything about the car screams luxury. "Nice car, Maddox."

"Thanks. It's a V8 Maybach. Limos always seem so showy."

"I guess you don't need to be showy when you've got so much big dick energy," I tease him.

He pulls me onto his lap. "Don't get sassy with me, gorgeous, or my big dick will get even harder than it already is and I'll have to take you over my knee. I'm supposed to be taking it easy with you, remember?"

I lean into him as he holds me close. I can feel the hardness of said big dick energy underneath me but I honestly feel too sore, too replete and too *used* in the best kind of way for anything other than just taking comfort from his all-encompassing warmth.

"This is your car from now on. If there's ever a need to go somewhere without me, which there shouldn't be. It's bullet-proof. On call 24/7. The driver is a Navy SEAL with executive protection agent training."

"What?" A disbelieving laugh escapes me.

"You can never be too careful," he says, in his grizzly bear voice.

Before I can protest that I have no need for such a thing, the car pulls to a stop and the SEAL has already opened the door for us.

Noah helps me out and I notice we're on Fifth Avenue, in one of the most expensive neighborhoods in the city. I guess I shouldn't be surprised.

I notice then that someone's next to us on the sidewalk. It's a small, elderly woman with a cane, slightly hunched-over and wearing a bright yellow headscarf. She stops walking and squints up at us. "Well, if it isn't Noah, my knight in shining armor."

Noah turns. "Enid." He sounds happy to see her, like she's an old, dear friend. "How are you? On your way back from Mabel's?"

"As a matter of fact, yes. I don't usually visit her in the evenings but her hairless cat Nigel snuck out onto the fire escape so I had to help her lure him back in. He wasn't wearing his sweater and she was afraid he'd catch a chill. He refused the cat treats but the little bastard came back inside for the filet mignon, so all's well that ends well."

Noah laughs. "Glad to hear it. Enid, this is Lucky. Lucky, my friend Enid."

Enid studies me for a few seconds. "Lucky, your mother is obviously a wise and whimsical woman. She chose the perfect name for you. I'd say without a doubt you're the luckiest girl in New York City, landing this one. He's a gem and a keeper. Take it from an old woman who's been married five times, to two duds, two shady philanderers and one love of my life: hang on to him with everything you've got."

"Well, thank you for that advice, Enid." I look up at Noah and he's grinning at me.

"Yeah, Lucky. Hang onto me with everything you've got." *Damn, the man is gorgeous.* To Enid, Noah says, "Can we help you get home, Enid?"

"Nope," she says. "I'd forgotten how beautiful the city is this time of night. I'm enjoying my stroll. You two enjoy your evening. I'm sure I'll bump into you again sometime."

"I hope so," Noah replies. "Have a good night, Enid."

Enid shuffles off.

Noah lifts me into his arms.

"Luckiest girl in the world, I tell you!" Enid calls after us.

Noah chuckles.

"What are you doing, Steel?"

He kisses me as he carries me through an extremely luxurious lobby and into an extremely luxurious elevator. "I'm a romantic, Irish. Of course I'm going to carry you over the threshold."

"What threshold?"

"The threshold to our future together. The thing is, when a Lucky Irish walks into your life, it's impossible to even think about letting her out of your sight for the rest of time. The only choice is to shower her with gifts while doing everything in your fucking power to make every single one of her wildest dreams come true. That's just the way it is. So buckle up, Sunshine. I haven't even gotten started."

I laugh but at the same time my heart breaks a little more. Maybe break is the wrong word. It's like there's a fissure in there, forcing open a part of me that was locked away for a long time. Hopefulness, maybe. Belief that all the beauty of life could be realized. *Love.*

It's making my head spin because it's happening so fast but *I love him so much.*

The elevator doors open into a stylish, no-expenses-spared foyer with thick, tinted glass windows on either side of it, a marble black and white checker-board floor and an over-the-top chandelier that could look at home in a Scottish Highlands hunting lodge. Noah punches a code into a keypad and the ornate carved wood-and-steel doors open.

Holy fuck.

His apartment is unreal. Expansive, airy and opulent beyond belief. The natural light is to-die-for. That's my first impression. My second is, it's a little stark. A little too rich-bachelor-pad-who's-hardly-ever-home. I could transform this space into something even more comfortable for him, and equally luxurious.

A wall of windows showcases a view of a twilight sky, a few treetops down below, with only a few hints that we're even in a city at all. We're high up. Outside, there's an enormous patio with a pool, a hot tub with lights that show the rising steam, and a covered outdoor seating area. "Not too shabby, Mr. Maddox."

"Thanks, Ms. Irish. I've been meaning to hire a high-end interior designer. Maybe you can help me with that. You can have free rein, we'll contact whatever the best design magazine is, get you the feature, and just like that you're on the map."

There he goes again, poking at all my secret wildest dreams, like he's so good at doing.

There's a buzz at the door. "That must be Bruce."

"Bruce?"

"My lawyer." Noah sets me carefully on the couch. "I would kiss you right now because you're so unbelievably beautiful it just about blows my head off, but that would get me rock hard again and I'm about to let my lawyer in. Before I do, let me just say that I'm right here by your side. Just say yes to all of this. Stay right here."

"All of what?"

Noah smirks but says nothing. He goes to the door to open it. A man who could only be a lawyer—and a very expensive one—strides in.

"Bruce Davis, meet Lucky Ashton."

I stand and shake his hand. Noah invites him over to the 12-seater dining room table next to the space-age chef's kitchen. Noah's arm is around me and he pulls out a chair for me, then pulls his chair close to mine so his thigh is pressed up against mine. None of this escapes his lawyer's attention.

"This is a substantially different offer to your earlier one, Noah," comments Bruce, if not concerned then at least curious.

"It's a more realistic offer," Noah tells him, his tone making very clear that he's serious. His grizzly bear has gone full Kodiak. "We plan to turn Ashton Holdings into a powerhouse. This price reflects its potential. Do you have the paperwork?"

Bruce takes the contract out of his briefcase and slides it across the table.

The wording is exactly the same as the scrawled note Noah wrote this morning. There are a few more pages of legal jargon. And spaces for both our signatures.

"Do you need to consult with your own lawyers, Ms. Ashton?" asks Bruce.

"No." I've never liked my company's lawyers, chosen of course by my father. They never seem like they're very good at their jobs.

Bruce nods. "I took the liberty of contacting your CFO for the bank deposit information. Once you sign, the money will be transferred into the Ashton Holdings' account within minutes. Do you have any questions?"

I look at Noah. "Are you sure you want to do this?"

"More sure than I've ever been about anything." The look on his face is so *in love* I can't bring myself to hesitate when it comes to anything about him.

I pick up the pen and sign it. Noah does the same.

Bruce keeps his expression strictly professional. Even if he quietly suspects that his client has lost his mind, he doesn't show it. He slides another pile of papers toward me. "This is the other paperwork you requested, Noah. The transaction has been made and the sale is final. Ms. Ashton, your deed."

"Deed? What deed?"

"Your apartment building," Bruce says.

"What apartment building?"

Noah nudges his shoulder against mine. "The one you live in. I bought it. In your name."

"You bought...the whole *building*?"

"Bruce has created a trust for you," Noah says. "We've called it Lucky Irish Holdings."

"A trust?" My brain can't keep up with what they're telling me.

"The trust gives you a layer of protection," Bruce explains. "I've also created an LLC for you. Lucky Irish Holdings now owns the corporation that owns the building. There are forty-seven other apartments in the building. Like yours, seven others are owned. Forty are rented. We've set it up so that the rent, lease, tax and maintenance payments are paid directly into your trust's bank account. After the property taxes, maintenance, upkeep expenses, and the salaries of the personnel, the trust will receive a monthly after-tax income of approximately five hundred thousand dollars."

"What?"

"All I need is your signature on pages three, seven, and twelve."

"How did you do all this?" I ask, mostly to Noah, but also to Bruce. "*Today?*"

Bruce takes this as a compliment. "My team works fast."

I stare at the stack of papers.

"If you prefer to have it looked over, that's fine," Bruce says. "But I can assure you it's airtight."

Just say yes.

I pick up the pen and sign on all three dotted lines. *What is this life?*

"That's everything, then." Bruce stands, gathers up the paperwork and starts putting it back into his briefcase.

Bruce shakes my hand, then Noah's, and heads for the door.

"It was nice meeting you, Lucky. Oh, and, Noah, Cash heard through the grapevine that Ashton Holdings was getting ready to accept a new offer."

"He heard about that?" Noah doesn't seem surprised.

"Yeah. And he, um…well, he heard that you might be involved in it, and he was fairly insistent about getting *all* the information out of me. You probably have a few missed calls. All three of your brothers are on their way over here."

36

As soon as the door closes behind Bruce, Noah turns to me. He gazes at me like I'm the only thing he can see and the only thing he cares about.

His palm slides along my jaw, weaving under my hair to grip the nape of my neck. It's a thing he does, a slow, powerful reminder of his strength and his barely-controlled vigor. Every time he does it, I go wet for him.

I love how handsome he is, how big and unashamedly rugged, even though he *shouldn't* be rugged. He can't help it. He's a ridiculously sexy, manly hunk, who'd fit in just as easily wrangling bucking broncos on some wild Wyoming ranch as he would in a Manhattan boardroom. It was one of the first things I noticed about him, and its effect only compounds itself.

Most of all, I love how he makes me feel alive in a way I've never experienced. He's woken up a part of me

—my lucky, Irish wild side—that was always hidden in there somewhere but never had a chance to find the light of day. Like a seed that, under his blazing August sun, has not only sprouted, but has found her full, noon-time bloom. "I can't believe you just did all that."

He kisses me. "My little dream girl is getting good at saying yes."

"When have I ever said no to you, Noah Steel?"

"I didn't want you to start now. I was prepared to go to a billion to knock those bad boys off your wildest dreams list."

"You're crazy." *He's a gem and a keeper. Hang on to him with everything you've got.* I already knew that, Enid, but thanks for the tip.

"Crazy for you, baby girl." His hand tangles in my hair, the other pulling me against his big, hard body.

"Your brothers are coming over?" I gasp.

"Sounds like it. Cash is probably going to blow a major gasket but just ignore him. I'd lock them out but Colton knows the code."

He claims me with his mouth, the kiss turning slippery and greedy.

We're so caught up in the kiss, it takes us a few seconds to register a sound. Of someone clearing his throat. "Eh-*ehm*. Hello-o-o." I recognize it as Colton's voice.

We break the kiss and turn to see…a whole bunch of people standing there staring at us. Taking in every detail of the way I'm practically wrapped around Noah and his hands are gripping my ass.

Slowly, we disengage. Noah's arm goes around me. His stance is protective, like he's shielding me. "To what do we owe the astounding pleasure of this unannounced visit by my entire family?" Noah asks sarcastically.

Cash is here, looking surly, with his arm around the waist of a gorgeous woman with wavy reddish-blond hair. Colton is grinning widely, holding the hand of another beautiful woman wearing the cutest dress. There's another man who could only be the oldest brother. He's tall and black-haired, almost prodigally handsome. He's got his arm slung around a petite woman with dark hair. She's exotic-looking and absolutely stunning.

Noah makes the introductions. "Lucky, you've met Cash and Colton. This is Dusty, Lila, Alexander and Ivy.

"So nice to meet you all."

Dusty steps forward and kisses my cheek. "It's such a pleasure to meet you, Lucky," she says with a big smile and a distinctly Texan twang. She's wearing a pink top and jeans that show off her gorgeous body, and cowgirl boots. "We've all been waiting for Noah to fall as hard and as fast as the rest of them. We *had* to come meet you."

Colton smiles and kisses Lila. "*I* fell the hardest." Then he holds up the large brown paper bag he's holding. "We brought dinner. Hope you lovebirds are hungry."

There's a lot of cheek-kissing as they all greet me.

Their banter and conversation flow easily, like only a close-knit family's can. Colton, Lila, Alexander and Ivy make their way over to the massive marble kitchen island and start setting out the food, laughing and groaning at Colton's terrible jokes.

Only Cash hangs back, and Dusty stays close to him. Cash is glaring at Noah. "Have you lost your mind?"

"Actually I've never felt more sane in my life, brother." Noah isn't fazed by Cash's bad mood in the slightest. This morning, it would have terrified me. Now, with Noah's reassurance still wrapped around me, it has no effect whatsoever. I can't feel bad about any of it.

"I should take you outside and pummel you into next week," Cash seethes.

"I'd like to see you try that," Noah laughs. "Things happened, none of which had anything to do with you."

Dusty winks at me, running her hand over Cash's shoulder. He immediately softens. They exchange a glance and it's almost comical watching Cash melt. It's easy to see that he's absolutely besotted. And I'm relieved. Under Dusty's influence, his rage is clearly being cooled by several degrees.

Noah's arm is still around me. "Lucky and I came to an agreement. Just the two of us. The offer you and I made together was already off the table. Shit happens, bro. Deal with it."

Colton laughs, entertained by the argument. The nearby kitchen group are obviously listening in.

"Colton invested an obscene amount of money in my business before I even *had* a business," Lila offers.

"Alexander bought my apartment building for me, only three days after we met," Ivy adds. Alexander grins at her, both wolfishly and adoringly.

"And Cash," Dusty says, kissing his cheek, "bought my mother's house for her, set up a recording deal for my sister and forced me to move in with him even though he was my boss."

Churlishly, Cash relents a little more. "I'm still your boss."

"Only at work," she teases him and his eyes narrow at her like he's thinking absolutely filthy thoughts.

Colton tucks a strand of Lila's hair behind her ear. "It's just the way we Maddoxes operate, Cash, you know that as well as anyone. You can hardly complain about it when Noah does the same thing."

Alexander's voice is deep and commanding, with a big-brother authority that pretty much settles the matter. "Cash, you wouldn't have a company to invest with at all if Noah hadn't saved your ass when you spent months dreamily googling 'Tex' while your business floundered."

Cash looks chagrinned for a milli-second, then he pulls Dusty closer. "I need to be consoled, Tex. My family is bullying me."

"Aw," she glides the backs of her fingers across his jaw. "It sucks when the bully gets bullied. You deserve all of it."

He kisses her. "You're in for it later," he murmurs.

Then he stands up and offers his hand to me. "I'm sorry, Lucky. I'm an asshole. I try not to be but it happens anyway. Please forgive me." I can't help smiling as I take his hand and he leans in to kiss my cheek. Then he offers his hand to Noah. "Dude, I'm just jealous. You two are going to make an absolute killing with Ashton Holdings. Your company is a little gem, Lucky."

"Thank you. I know it is."

With that, the tension is completely gone, all is forgiven and dinner is served. We sit outside on the huge, private patio and I find myself in a whirlwind of fun and getting to know them all.

As an only child with parents who were either gone or almost entirely absent, it's so new to be around such a boisterous, loving family.

And that's what they are. A *family*.

I'm a little quieter than the rest of them, but it's so fascinating to me to watch their kindness with each other, their genuine, bone-deep friendship and their easy laughter. I'm sort of falling in love with all of them.

It turns out Lila is Lila *Bailey*, the up and coming designer everyone is talking about. When I tell her I recently bought one of her tops and it's my favorite piece of clothing, she invites me to come into her design studio and choose anything I like.

Colton, as always, is the life of the party. He satellites around Lila, touching her, smoothing her hair, kissing her and generally being so in love with her it's wildly enter-taining to watch. The two of them banter constantly and have everyone laughing. They tell me the story of how they met at a party and he insisted on driving her to her friend's wedding in L.A. in a fancy tour bus, and then they ended up getting married (and pregnant) in Vegas.

I'm also amazed to learn that Ivy is Ivy *Laine*. She's one of my favorite musicians. She hugs me when I tell her I love her music and have been listening to her new album on repeat. She's so humble and beautiful it's impossible not to love her.

Alexander watches Ivy like a man obsessed. Ivy is also pregnant, and a little further along than Lila. The two of them tell me the story of how they met on a fake date and Alexander is so honest and funny about how fast he fell for her it makes me smile.

Dusty is outgoing and easy to get to know, and Cash is a very different person to the intimidating boardroom shark when he's around her. He's relaxed and so smitten, his humility shines through. It turns out to be impossible not to love him for it.

And Noah is…*mine*. I've given up trying to analyze it. When you know, you know, and sometimes that's enough.

After we've finished eating dinner, he pulls me onto his lap. His strong arms hold me and I lean into him, breathing in his minty, woodsy scent that's become so familiar. "You okay, Irish?" he murmurs.

"Very okay. Are you?"

He slowly shakes his head.

I touch my fingers to his stubbled jaw. "Why not?"

He whispers in my ear as the others laugh at something one of them said. "You're so beautiful my heart hurts."

I haven't said the words in a very long time. They were locked away until Noah broke my heart wide open. I lean close to him and whisper back, "I love you."

LATER, after Noah's family leaves, he carries me upstairs. His bedroom is absolutely palatial, and very minimalistic. A tinted glass wall opens out onto another large balcony. The only piece of furniture in the room is a massive bed.

He lays me onto it, crouching over me, laying himself onto me but holding his weight.

My hands cup his face. "I love your family."

"They love you. And I love you more."

My connection to Noah Maddox has wrapped itself around me and become one with my life on so many levels and in such a short amount of time, I don't know how to feel, except very, very in love with him. "I love you too, Noah."

"Lucky?"

"Yeah?"

"It's fast, I know that. I can't slow it down and I don't want to. I'm in love with you. I'm in love with the fire in your eyes and your spunky sweetness. I'm in love with your crazy beauty and the way you felt like mine from the first second I laid eyes on you. *Before* I even laid eyes on you. I think I loved you the first time I saw your picture on that app. I don't want to rush you, but I'm going to buy you the ring of your wildest dreams and then I'm going to ask you to marry me. When you're ready."

I never did manage to get the bracelet he gave me to unclasp. It fits perfectly and seems to want to live right where it is. "I'll probably say yes. When I'm ready."

"Maybe next weekend."

We laugh because it's so unlikely but it feels so achingly right. "I might *have* to marry you if I don't start googling soon."

He gazes down at me so tenderly I fall fall fall. "What are you going to google? Magical baby?"

The words do something to us both. My logical mind is *zero* match for the rush of lust and need that courses through my veins. Noah kisses me as his *huge*, thick hardness presses against the soft wetness of my pussy through the thin layer of my dress.

We're obviously rushing everything. We have from the very beginning. But when something feels this good and *this* sure of itself, the most beautiful of choices make themselves.

Noah unties my wrap dress and takes off my bra and

my panties. He kisses my breasts, nuzzling my nipples, sucking on one, then the other until I'm moaning.

He kisses his way down my stomach, pinning my legs wide. His mouth latches onto me, licking into me, feasting on me like he's addicted. *"You're the sweetest thing, my Lucky Irish. You're mine."*

My fingers weave into the thick silk of his hair as I give myself to him fully. He sucks on my clit until I'm shattering in tight, clenching bursts as I cry his name.

When the ripples begin to calm, he climbs up my body and uses the wetness to ease his massive cock's entry, driving deep inside me, forcing me to take all of him. He feels like hot, thick magic, stretching me, pressing and rubbing, driving into me with possessive strokes that give me no choice but to take all of him. I wrap my arms and my legs around him as he whispers sweet words to me. *I love how you feel. You're the most beautiful thing that's ever happened to me.*

Until the orgasm becomes the highest and most intense one yet. The pleasure isn't just physical, but whole-souled. My emotions and my cravings wrap themselves just a little more tightly around this man who has swept me away in the truest sense of the word. He takes me again to the heights of what I can handle, filling me to the brim with his flooding heat until my body is squeezing and drawing as much of him inside as I can take. Until I'm overflowing with his seed and the pleasure overload he insists on.

And when we slowly start to come down from all that, he says, "Stay with me tonight. And tomorrow night. And the night after. We'll figure everything else out. Just say yes, Irish."

And so I do.

EPILOGUE

Lucky

Four months later

"THIS DRESS IS ABSOLUTELY STUNNING, Lucky. Lila, you've totally outdone yourself," Dusty gushes as she adjusts my veil. "Lucky, you're the most beautiful bride I've ever seen. And the baby bump only adds to the whole effect."

"So do all of yours." I blot tears from my eyes so I don't ruin my make-up. One thing about being pregnant, you feel like your emotions are on overdrive. My joy keeps overflowing. "Lila, I love it so much." My wedding dress is one of Lila's own designs. It has a gorgeous fitted white lace bodice and a full skirt made entirely of white feathers. "I don't know how you did this." I've just started showing, now that I'm four months along.

"I wanted you to have something special," she says, helping Dusty make sure my veil sits just right. Embroi-

263

dered into the lace are two linked hearts and a shamrock. "Noah's going to lose his mind when he sees you."

"He's already lost his mind," Grace laughs.

It's true my gorgeous fiancé tends to be almost manically protective of me, especially since we found out that we did, in fact, conceive our magical baby that first weekend we spent together. I started getting morning sickness only a week or two later. I already love this baby so much I can hardly handle it. I'm *happy* in a way I've never been.

I'm sure I didn't intentionally set out to start working on that particular wildest dream the night I met Noah. But something in me leaned in. Something in him leaned in too. When I took the pregnancy test and we saw it was positive, we both cried. And if you don't think it amps the hormones into hyperdrive when your hot, manly, beast-in-bed billionaire fiancé has tears in his eyes because he's so overjoyed he's going to be a Daddy, trust me, it does. We spent the entire day acting like we were trying to conceive that baby all over again.

The night before I took the pregnancy test, Noah had Tiffany's open just for the two of us. He told me to pick the ring I liked best. Any one I wanted. *For when you're ready,* he said. I said I was already ready so he got down on one knee and proposed to me right there in the middle of Tiffany's. I said yes.

I didn't know it was possible for love to compound

itself like it does when I'm with him, but I fall deeper in love with my husband-to-be every day.

It's still a little hard to believe that we just *knew*. We jumped straight into the deep end before we even knew each other's real last names. Grace says I manifested Noah that night she created my dating profile and that the universe delivered. I've decided to believe her, because only the most potent kind of luck-dusted magic could have brought Noah Maddox into my life.

Noah came with me for my first scan. The doctor asked us if we wanted to know what we were having and we both said yes. It's a girl. We could see her strong little heart beating. It was one of the most beautiful moments of my life. We're going to name her Maeve. After my mother.

As an engagement present, Noah took me to Ireland and surprised me with a piece of land he bought for us in County Cork. It's the most idyllic place. Just green fields as far as the eye can see. It's on the coast with views of the ocean. We're going to build a house there, designed just the way we want it. The day we were there, a double rainbow appeared over the fields and it was the brightest one I've ever seen. It was the kind of thing that makes you believe that pots of gold really do exist. I've found mine. He's a sexy, living, breathing pot of gold and I'm keeping him.

Last week, Noah flew everyone to his—our—house in

Italy to get ready for our wedding. Turns out he—*we*—have a lot of houses. I haven't even seen half of them yet.

The Italian villa overlooks Lake Como, has twelve bedrooms and a large, ornate, covered patio with stunning views of the water and the mountains. Steps lead down to a boathouse and our own private beach.

We're having a small wedding, since I don't have family—aside from the cousins and second cousins in Ireland, who were absolutely thrilled we bought land there and had a party for us at one of the local pubs when we visited. It's going to be fun getting to know them.

Alexander and Ivy are here, Colton and Lila, Cash and Dusty, Grace and Ethan, and Enid and Mabel.

Noah flew Enid and Mabel to Italy for an all-expenses-paid two week trip (we found a cat sitter for Nigel), since neither one of them had ever been out of the United States. After the wedding they're going to visit Rome, Florence and Venice. They're having the time of their lives. The two of them are a total hoot, like a comedy duo. We kept running into Enid on her walks and we invited her to dinner one night. She's had the most fascinating life and she hands out snippets of wise advice that are genuinely sort of life-changing. She's become a dear friend.

My sisters-in-law-to-be have become my best friends. I couldn't love them more. Dusty is down-to-earth and so easy to talk to, we have long talks about everything under the sun. We talk on the phone every day, often several times a day. Lila is an absolute sweetheart and goes out of her way to be there for me. She's an only child too and we click over so many things. She's always gifting me with pieces of clothing I love and I value her friendship more than I can express. Ivy is one of the most talented people I've ever met. She's kind and soulful, beautiful inside and out, and I just adore her.

And my new brothers-in-law are so charming and fun, I love being around them.

Grace and I have become closer than ever. She moved in with Ethan the same weekend I moved in with Noah. He asked her to marry him at the top of the Empire State Building less than three months after they met. They plan to have a small ceremony next month and have booked Hopeless Romantic for their reception.

All four of my bridesmaids are also expecting babies. The Maddox brothers joke that there's something in the water, but we all know it has nothing to do with water and everything to do with…well, all I know is that *my* Maddox brother has been very thorough about doing his best to make sure that particular wildest dream has come true.

Ivy's due in less than a month, Lila has another two months before her due date, Dusty found out she was pregnant soon after I did, and Grace found out the day after she arrived in Italy.

I never did go back to my apartment. Not to sleep, anyway. Now I use it as my office.

With his encouragement, I started decorating Noah's

—*our*—apartment the day after I moved in. It took me a few months to get it done since it's so big, but we're both thrilled with the way it turned out. True to his word, Noah organized features in ten of the top home design magazines in New York.

Since then, I've had a *lot* of requests from people wanting an interior designer. Noah doesn't want me working too much and I agree. I would never do anything to make my pregnancy more risky than it needs to be. I've decided to take on three or four projects a year. I'll choose only the projects I'm most passionate about—and, as Noah suggested—pay absolute top dollar.

Ashton Holdings has doubled in value over the past four months. Getting a very substantial cash injection, of course, helped. Having Noah as my "consultant" has also made a huge difference. He's incredibly knowledgeable and he's also good with people. We restructured the business, gave (very generous) redundancy packages to the older Board members who didn't mesh with our new vision, and hired some young, smart analysts who have injected new life into the company culture. Noah told me about the "creative week" Invested Enterprises offers its staff and we've just started doing something similar, where people can travel, discover new opportunities and meet fresh talent. So far it's going really well. The word's gotten out and we're now getting hundreds of new applicants each week.

Noah convinced me to hire a co-CEO, or at least

that's her title. The reality is that she's taken on most of the job and I act as her consultant. Her name is Ella Bond and she's absolutely fantastic. She's so smart, capable and reliable it's taken all the stress out of the equation.

"Lucky, it's time." Ivy hands me my bouquet of white roses, beaming at me. The string quartet is starting up out on the patio. Alexander comes up behind Ivy and kisses her neck.

"Wow, Lucky," he says. "You're absolutely stunning. My brother is a lucky man. Are you ready?"

I nod. Alexander is giving me away. He offered and I liked the idea. I know my father is looking down at me from wherever he is, at my mother's side. He would have been happy about the way we've turned the business around. And the way everything has turned out. But it's my mother's spirit I can feel most of all. I can't help but sense that she somehow led me to Noah.

Each of my bridesmaids gives me a kiss on the cheek. Then they take their places, leading our way. Alexander offers his arm for me to hold. "You've made him so happy, Lucky."

"He's made me happier than I knew I could be." *He's made all my wildest dreams come true.*

The wedding march plays and I hold onto Alexander's arm like I'm in a dream.

Noah is standing by a flower-decorated altar. Cash and Colton stand next to him, and a minister.

Noah looks beyond handsome in his tux, his hair lightly tousled by the breeze off the lake, his eyes as blue as I've ever seen them.

I love him so much.

He's smiling at me, so gorgeous I can't believe he's real.

Alexander takes my hand and places it in Noah's. "Congratulations, you two." Then he takes his place beside his brothers.

Noah lifts my veil. "You're the most beautiful thing I've ever seen, Lucky Irish."

He holds both my hands and we gaze into each other's eyes, as in love as it's possible to be.

The minister begins.

We recite our handwritten vows under the Italian sun, surrounded by our family.

"Do you, Noah Patrick Sullivan Maddox, take Lucky Emerson O'Callahan Ashton to be your lawfully wedded wife?"

"Hell, yes. I do."

"And do you, Lucky Emerson O'Callahan Ashton, take Noah Patrick Sullivan Maddox to be your lawfully wedded husband?"

"Yes." *Yes yes yes yes yes.* "I do."

Thank you so much for reading **Billionaire Romantic**.

If you enjoyed this book, please consider leaving a quick review or rating on Amazon.

Want to see what happens with Noah and Lucky a year and a half —and ten years—down the road? Get the free bonus epilogue here: https://BookHip.com/BKFVXWZ

Below I've included the first chapter of **Billionaire Boss,** the first standalone book in the **New York Billionaires** series, starring Cash and Dusty.

xoxo,

Julie

Please come join my Facebook reader group, Julie Capulet's Romantics, where I share cover reveals, insider info and we discuss all things romance!

Sign up for my newsletter to receive my free bonus content and get access to sneak peeks and exclusive giveaways!

Visit my website @ www.juliecapulet.com

Our deal was simple. One night. Fake names. No strings attached.

Until it turns out he's my new boss...

I couldn't believe my luck when I got sent to a work conference in Hawaii. Living the dream after years of pulling myself up by my bootstraps.

The sand, the palm trees and the blue water were straight out of a romantic fantasy. So was the guy at the beachfront bar, let's be honest. Blue eyes. Broad-shouldered in his business suit but with a rough-around-the-edges swagger and a filthy mouth.

We laughed and had a night of crazy passion that enlightened me in every possible way. I understood what dreams coming true might actually feel like.

And then I left without saying goodbye.

That was two months ago and I've mostly been able to

put him out of my mind. I've been busy landing my dream job in New York City.

Imagine my surprise when my new boss turns out to be Mr. Dirty Talking Swagger.

He's been thinking about me too, he says, his blue eyes dancing. He's been searching for me since that night.

And he wants to see me in his office…

Billionaire Boss is a steamy contemporary billionaire romance and the first book in the New York Billionaires series, starring the four Maddox brothers. Each book in the series is a complete standalone with an HEA.

New York Billionaires

Chapter One

"This is your hotel here, Dusty." My Uber driver, Earl, who I've learned on the twelve minute ride in from the Honolulu airport has been married to his high school sweetheart Marion for twenty-seven years, retired to Hawaii three years ago after Marion decided she could no longer handle the brutal Pittsburgh winters, has five grandchildren who visit for two weeks every Christmas and, as much as he loves seeing them, is always relieved when it's time for them to go. I even know their names: Huck, Brodie, Cassandra, Milo and Imogen. "It's the best hotel in Waikiki. No contest."

We pull up outside an unbelievably luxurious hotel with tall columns and a welcoming row of stately palm trees. The scene is as picture perfect as…well, as a life-long fantasy of being sent to Hawaii for a fully paid-for work trip can be.

Travel brochures and marathon binges of Hawaii Life don't really capture the neon turquoise of the water. Or the ideal temperature of the balmy, sea-scented air.

This place is unreal.

"Just wait until you see the views once you get inside," Earl tells me. "You're in for a treat. This is the oldest hotel in Oahu. The two towers on either side of the main building are the new additions, but the original hotel is where the charm is. The whole place is pure luxury."

"It's right on the beach?"

"Sure is. Best waterfront bar in Waikiki, hands down. An absolute magnet for love birds. I'm always giving rides to couples who are coming back to celebrate the place they first met, at least once a week. They're on their honeymoons, or they're here to celebrate their fifth, tenth or twenty-fifth wedding anniversaries. I once had this older couple coming back for their fiftieth. It's as if this place is spiking its drinks with aphrodisiacs and love potions. And you have that look to you." He winks at me in the rear view mirror.

"What look?"

"The starstruck one. The one that tells me your life is about to change."

I laugh lightly. "Oh, no, I'm just here for a conference."

"That's what they all say." He grins at me, then gets out to retrieve my bags.

I wriggle myself out of the backseat of the cab, no mean feat in the tight pencil skirt I poured myself into ten grueling hours ago. It was clearly the wrong choice for a hellish day of travel, but this is my first ever work trip and I was hoping to give the first impression of a put-together professional—a slightly crumpled one at this point, after a commuter flight from Austin to Houston, then eight and a half hours to Honolulu. I couldn't really rock up to the business class lounge in my usual jeans and cowboy boots, as tempting as that might have been. If I want to be taken seriously as a newly-minted financial advisor, straight out of college and fighting her way to the top of a dog-eat-dog, heavily male-dominated scene, I at least need to look the part.

I thank Earl, giving my best to Marion, Huck, Brodie, Cassandra, Milo and especially Imogen (who suffers from stage fright and has a piano recital next Thursday), immediately rate him five stars and give him a huge tip. "Bye, Earl."

"See you on your honeymoon," he winks.

I smile and wave as he drives away. Good old Earl.

As much as Earl might think of himself as an oracle, I laugh off his prediction. For better or worse, the circumstances of my life have made me a die-hard realist. Any romantic tendencies I might have been born with got trampled by ambition and circumstance a long time ago.

I heave my gigantic suitcase—because I've never been on a work trip *or* to Hawaii and you never know what you might need—up the ramp. God bless the genius who invented wheeled suitcases, is all I can say.

Walking into the lobby of the hotel, I have to stop for a minute just to take in the breath-taking view.

Woah.

There's a giant banyan tree (thank you, three a.m. googling sessions) in the middle of a scenic, wide-open courtyard. A glittering pool sits to its right and there's a restaurant with a colorfully-lit stage, even in broad daylight, where a musician is singing a Hawaiian classic I recognize.

Somewhere Over the Rainbow.

You can say that again.

It's so beautiful I feel like I'm hallucinating.

The bar is perfectly positioned under the majestic tree. Beyond that, the golden sand of Waikiki Beach and the twinkling blue water are as idyllic as a fantasy.

"Pretty spectacular, huh?"

A man is standing next to me. He's dressed in a suit and has reddish, thinning hair and eyes so pale blue he almost looks see-through. He checks me out before his gaze lands once again on my face.

Um, no.

"Are you here for the conference? I'm Brad Channing. I'm with Rothwell and Dodd Financials."

"Oh. That's…nice."

I'm beyond grateful when two of his colleagues walk over and hand him his key card. "Ogilvie wants to meet with us pronto," one of them says to him.

I take that as my cue to flee. "I better check in. Enjoy your stay." I make a beeline for the check-in desk before Brad can corner me with more chitchat. He glances back at me as he follows his colleagues outside.

Not a chance in hell, Brad. I'm definitely not here to get picked up by a junior assistant in a bad suit. My ambitions are on overdrive. Besides, I have way too much to achieve to get bogged down by a relationship, no matter what Earl might have joked about.

I wait in the check-in line. The hotel is busy with happy, relaxed people. Some are obviously here for the conference and are dressed in now-wrinkled business clothes, but most of the guests are wearing bathing suits and tropical prints. The more suntanned they are, the more relaxed they seem to be.

As I wait, I gaze out past the row of rocking chairs that line the deck, where people are reading books and sipping cocktails, to the beach and the cluster of surfers in the distance, catching wave after perfect wave. I'm already counting down the minutes until I can slip into my bikini and immerse myself blissfully into that blue, blue water.

I still can't believe this is *real.* I've flown business class to one of the most beautiful places in the world without having to pay a cent for any of it. In fact I'm being *paid* to be here.

Until a few hours ago, I'd only been out of the state of Texas once in my life.

The truth is, the struggles I watched my mother deal with my entire life have been implanted in my brain by now, and they motivate me to work like nothing else could, until the universe has no choice but to hoist me out of the rut my family seems to have been mired in for a long time. After my dad went AWOL when I was four years old, my mom and my older sister Skylar and I moved into our tiny bungalow in a lower-rent neighborhood (at the time, at least) of central Austin where my mother has lived ever since. She spent my childhood working day and night to meet our very basic needs. Both

Sky and I started working as soon as we were old enough to help her.

And she did meet our basic needs. After searching for my dad but always coming up empty, she finally gave up. We later found out he'd changed his name—what a hero—then died in a drunk driving accident two years later.

So we made it work on our own, because we had no choice.

It was a struggle. We never had any extras. My mom used to make light of it and call it our no-frills lifestyle. We ate what we could afford, we had one pair of shoes each and we bought our clothes from thrift stores. When my friends took trips to Europe and vacationed in the Bahamas, I stayed at home with my paper route. When my classmates bought all the latest gadgets, I watched them play with them. And as I did, I set goals.

I read somewhere that you're 43% more likely to achieve your goals if you write them down. The room I shared with my sister was so decorated with Post-it notes, she complained. I started a dog-walking business when I was seven. I got a paper route when I was ten. I got a job in a coffee shop when I was twelve, working under the table until I turned fourteen. When I wasn't working, I was studying.

UT was within walking distance to our house, so I started going to the library there when I was in sixth grade, skimming my fingers along the rows of books, watching the college students with their stuffed-full tote bags, their shiny MacBooks and their colorful Longhorns merch. I vowed I would not only get accepted into UT, but also put myself through college, graduate near the top of my class, and land myself a job that would pay me enough money to help my family and make sure we no longer had to struggle so damn hard every single day of our lives.

And I've *done* it.

The way the sunlight is sparkling on the white-capped blue waves is reminding me that all my hard work has finally paid off.

My new job might not be perfect but it's one step closer to the security I've always craved. My next goal: to land my dream job in New York City.

I visited my roommate from college in New York the summer after my freshman year and completely fell in love with the energy and the buzz of the place. I was enchanted by the look of it and the glamour. The opportunities to build something incredible out of your life had me hooked—that feeling that you're in the center of the world, where anything can happen. You could *feel* every lyric to all the songs that have been written about New York City. *Concrete jungle where dreams are made of. There's nothing you can't do. It's up to you, New York New York.* I wanted to be a part of it so badly I could taste it.

So I've been working my heart out every day since to get there.

"Next." The woman behind the desk smiles.

I step forward. "I have a reservation under Rose. Dusty Rose. I'm here for the Emerging Into Investments conference."

The receptionist types in my information. "You're here with Stellar Investments?"

"Yes, that's right."

"I'll just need your ID. The room is fully pre-paid."

She types in my info, sliding two plastic cards into an envelope. "Welcome to Hawaii, Ms. Rose. Your room is on the fourth floor. Number 417. Courtyard view, which is the best view, in my opinion. Here's your key and this card is a towel voucher. Swap it for a towel at the desk next to the pool and when you return it they'll give you a new card. Here's the finalized agenda for the conference, which is being held right across the street. And here's some information about the excursions and activities we offer if you have some downtime. Wi-Fi is complimentary and the elevator is right over there. Enjoy your stay."

"Thank you." My heart feels so full it might burst.

I find my way to the elevator, pressing the button for the fourth floor, charmed all over again by the surreal scene outside the open doors of the foyer, which leads to a bar area where a grand piano sits.

As the elevator takes me up, I scan the conference agenda. It's a two-day event with a jam-packed line-up of speakers, starting first thing tomorrow morning. At four-thirty each afternoon, the conference winds down, replaced by a cocktail hour.

My room is as beautiful as the rest of the hotel. There's a king-sized bed and tropical-themed art on the walls. Open French doors are framed by plantation-style shutters, leading out to a tiny Juliet-style balcony that looks out over the courtyard and beach. I can hear the live music.

After all the hours of studying, the exhausting internships, the working two jobs to pay my way through college: all of it—right here and right now—finally feels worth it.

For a second I just take it all in, wondering what it *would* feel like to come back here on your one-year anniversary, or your twenty-fifth. To revisit this magical place and reminisce about that one weekend where it all began.

You've got that look to you.

I laugh to myself.

Sure I do.

Putting on my bikini, I tie a pink hibiscus-print wrap dress over it and head for the beach.

ALSO BY JULIE CAPULET

I Love You Series

The Obsession Begins (free)

XOXO I Love You

XOXX I Love You More

Love You the Most (free)

Sexy Standalones

Max

Cowboy

McCabe Brothers Series

Hopeless Romantic

My Hero

Arrogant Player

Music City Lovers Series

Nashville Days

Nashville Nights

Nashville Dreams

Nashville Lights

Hawthorne U Series

Lovestruck

Paradise Series

Devil's Angel

Wild Hearts

New York Billionaires Series

Billionaire Boss

Billionaire Grump

Billionaire Devil

Billionaire Romantic

Standalone Rom-com

Beautiful Savages

ABOUT THE AUTHOR

Julie Capulet is an Amazon top 20 bestselling author of contemporary romance. She writes steamy he-falls-first romance with heart, heat and fairy tale HEAs. Her stories are inspired by true love and she's married to her own real life hero. When she's not writing, she's reading, traveling, walking on the beach and watching rom-coms.

www.juliecapulet.com

www.ingramcontent.com/pod-product-compliance
Lightning Source LLC
Chambersburg PA
CBHW020129310726
48970CB00006B/1793